MACMILL[illegible]
INTERMED[illegible]

JANE AUSTEN

Sense and Sensibility

Retold by Elizabeth Walker

INTERMEDIATE LEVEL

Founding Editor: John Milne

The Macmillan Readers provide a choice of enjoyable reading materials for learners of English. The series is published at six levels – Starter, Beginner, Elementary, Pre-intermediate, Intermediate and Upper.

Level control
Information, structure and vocabulary are controlled to suit the students' ability at each level.

The number of words at each level:

Starter	about 300 basic words
Beginner	about 600 basic words
Elementary	about 1100 basic words
Pre-intermediate	about 1400 basic words
Intermediate	about 1600 basic words
Upper	about 2200 basic words

Vocabulary
Some difficult words and phrases in this book are important for understanding the story. Some of these words are explained in the story and some are shown in the pictures. From Pre-intermediate level upwards, words are marked with a number like this: …[3]. These words are explained in the Glossary at the end of the book.

Answer keys
Answer keys for the *Points for Understanding* and the *Exercises* sections can be found at www.macmillanenglish.com

Contents

A Note About the Author and Life in the Nineteenth Century

Jane Austen was born on 16th December, 1775 at Steventon, Hampshire – a county[1] in the south of England. Jane's father was a clergyman[2] in the church at Steventon. Jane had six brothers – James, George, Edward, Henry and Charles – and one sister – Cassandra. Jane Austen's father made sure that his children had a good education. Jane learnt French, Italian and music. She studied English literature and poetry.

In 1803, Mr Austen and his family moved to Bath, a town in the west of England. Bath was popular and fashionable in the nineteenth century. People went there to meet friends. They played games of cards, and danced at balls in large buildings called The Assembly Rooms. They listened to music and watched plays in the theatres. They bought jewels and fashionable clothes in the shops. They walked in the wide streets and fine parks[3].

In 1805, Jane Austen's father died and the family moved to Southampton, in Hampshire. They lived there for only a few years. In 1810, the family moved again, to Chawton, in Hampshire. From that year, until her death in 1817, Jane was very busy. She wrote books, she visited her relatives[4], and she travelled round England with friends. Jane's brother, Edward, lived with Thomas and Catherine Knight. Mr and Mrs Knight had a large house – Godmersham Park – in the county of Kent. Jane and her sister often visited Edward at Godmersham Park. From her diaries and letters we can see that Jane was a very kind and intelligent woman.

Jane Austen never got married. Some people think that she fell in love in 1801, but the love affair did not end well. The young man did not have any money and they could not marry. Her lover died suddenly, a few years later.

In 1802, Harris Bigg-Wither asked Jane Austen to marry him. However, Jane and Harris were engaged for only one day. The following morning, Jane changed her mind[5]. She decided not to marry Mr Bigg-Wither.

In 1811, Jane Austen's first book was published. Not many women writers were published at this time. Publishers did not like publishing books by women. For this reason, many women writers used men's names when they wrote books. However, Jane Austen never used a man's name. Her books were published using her own name and her stories were extremely popular. Her books are: *Sense and Sensibility* (1811), *Pride and Prejudice* (1813), *Mansfield Park* (1814), *Emma* (1815), *Northanger Abbey* (1818), *Persuasion* (1818) and *Sanditon* (unfinished).

Jane Austen's stories were not about poor people. She wrote about people who had money and property – houses and land. These very rich and powerful people were the 'polite society' of Britain. Few people from polite society worked to earn money. Men inherited[6] money and property from their fathers. The eldest son usually received most of the money and property after his father's death. If younger sons did not choose to join the army, or the navy, they became lawyers or clergymen.

People in polite society spent a lot of time calling on each other – visiting each others' houses. Each person who called at the house of a friend, left a visiting card[7]. A servant then passed the card to the owner of the house. It was very impolite to call and not leave a visiting card, if the owner of the house was out.

People in polite society had dinner parties and dances in their homes. They played music and read books. They had conversations about art, music, poetry and politics. Men went out onto their land to hunt with dogs and guns. Women read poetry and they painted pictures. They also walked in the gardens, or they rode horses in the grounds of their large properties. In winter, men and women from polite society often left their country houses and stayed in London for a few months. In London they called on friends. They also enjoyed visiting fashionable places, and spending money.

Young women hoped to meet a suitable[8] young man in London and get married. It was important for a girl to marry a man who had money and property. If a girl did not have any money of her own and she did not marry, her life was much more difficult.

Good manners – the correct way that people behaved and spoke – were very important. Well-educated people, who had good manners, spoke quietly and intelligently. They thought about other peoples' feelings and they made sure that they did not upset them.

Men and women in polite society talked about each other in a formal way. They used the titles: *Lord*, *Sir*, *Mr*, *Mrs* or *Miss* in front of their last names. If they did not know the members of a family very well, people used *Miss* (+ their last name) when they spoke to elder, unmarried daughters. And they used *Miss* (+ their first name) when they spoke to younger, unmarried daughters. For example, the three young sisters in this story would be: Miss Dashwood, Miss Marianne and Miss Margaret. Married women would often be called by their husband's name. For example: Mrs John Dashwood. Men often used only their last names when they spoke about each other. For example: Brandon, or Ferrars.

Young women had to be introduced to young men whom they did not know. After that, they could talk to them. In polite society, women did not travel alone or visit places alone.

There were no cars, or trains, or bicycles at this time. People travelled in carriages pulled by horses, or they rode horses, or they walked.

NOTE: Willoughby is pronounced **will-o-bee**.

The Places in This Story

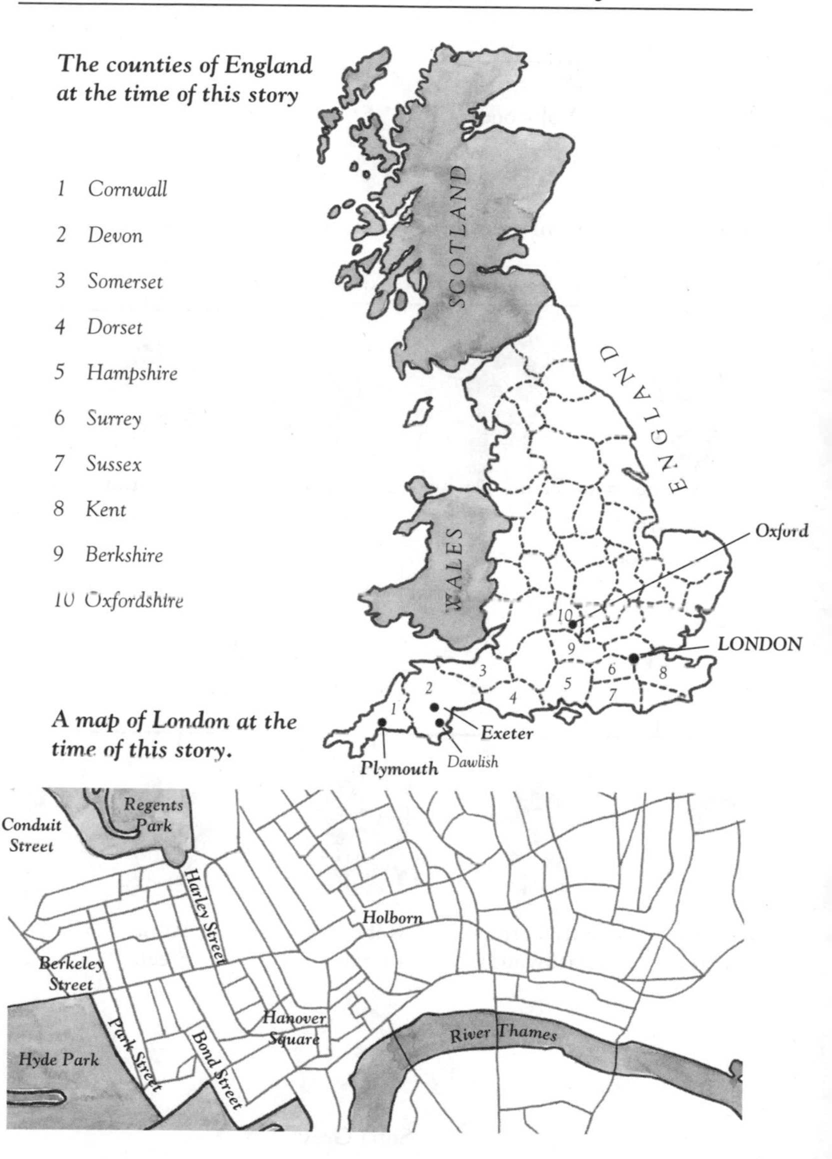

The People in This Story

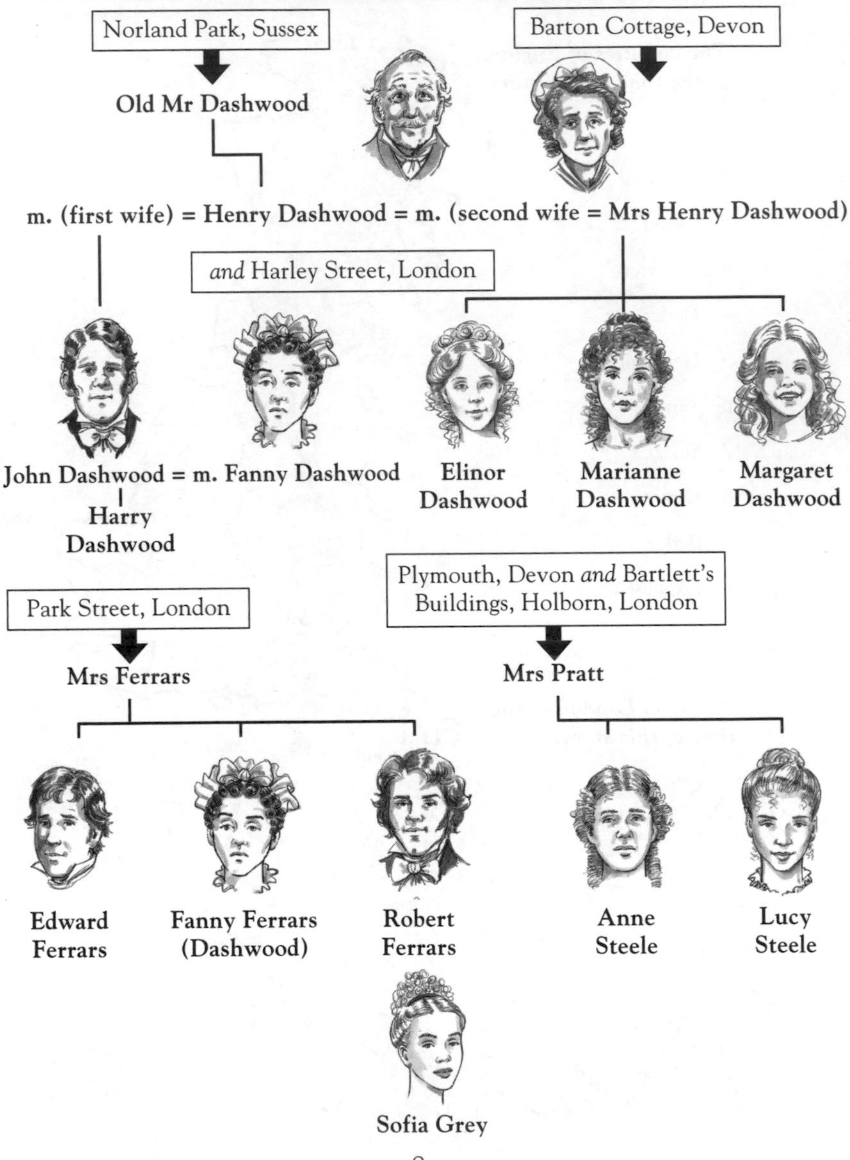

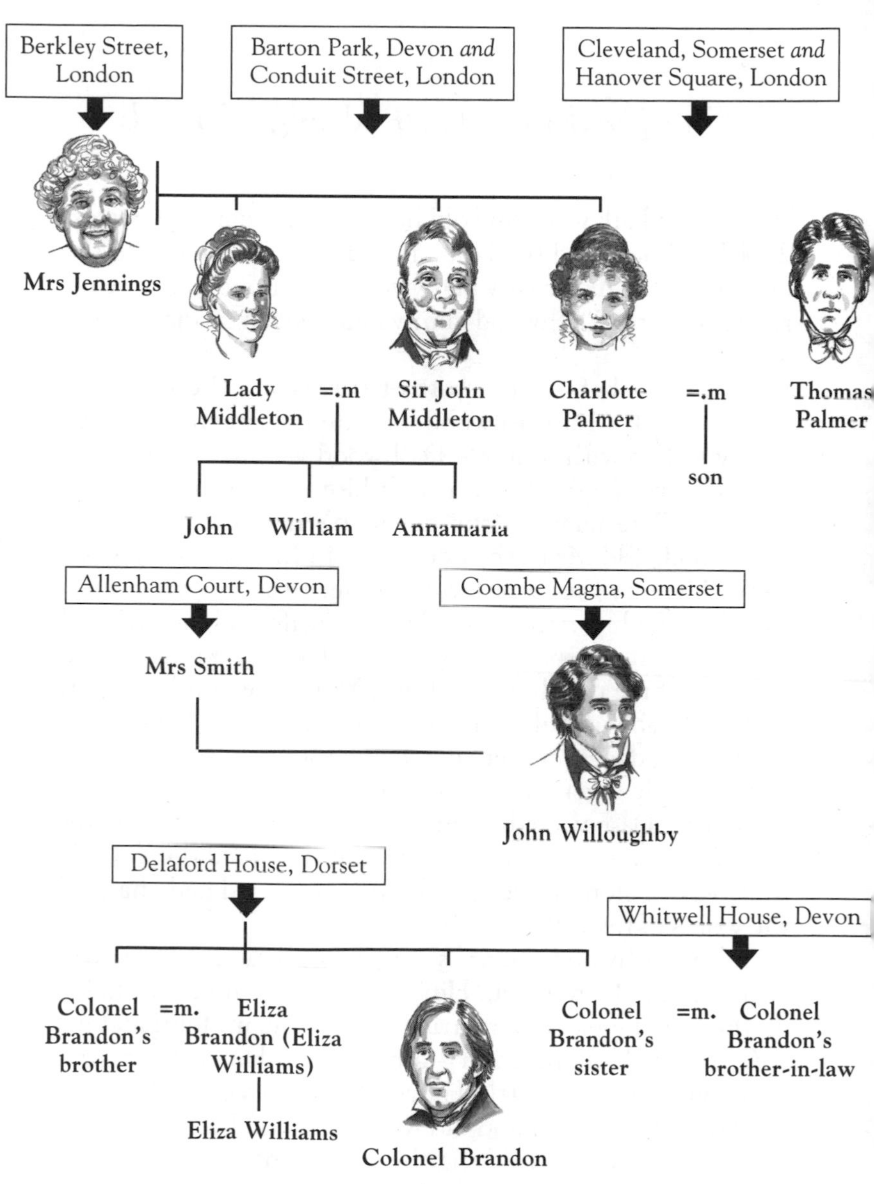
Berkley Street, London
Barton Park, Devon *and* Conduit Street, London
Cleveland, Somerset *and* Hanover Square, London
Mrs Jennings
Lady Middleton
=.m
Sir John Middleton
Charlotte Palmer
=.m
Thomas Palmer
son
John
William
Annamaria
Allenham Court, Devon
Coombe Magna, Somerset
Mrs Smith
John Willoughby
Delaford House, Dorset
Whitwell House, Devon
Colonel Brandon's brother
=m.
Eliza Brandon (Eliza Williams)
Eliza Williams
Colonel Brandon
Colonel Brandon's sister
=m.
Colonel Brandon's brother-in-law

1

The Dashwoods of Norland Park

Norland Park was a fine old house in the county of Sussex. The house and the land around it had belonged to the Dashwood family for very many years. For hundreds of years, members of the Dashwood family had lived at Norland Park.

Eleven years before the start of this story, the owner of Norland Park – Mr Dashwood – invited his nephew and his family to live with him. Mr Dashwood was an old man and he had never married and had children, so his nephew was his heir[9]. The name of the old man's nephew was Henry Dashwood. Old Mr Dashwood wrote in his will[10] that when he died, Henry Dashwood would inherit the property.

Henry had married twice. His first wife had died several years after their son, John, was born. Henry and his second wife had three daughters – Elinor, Marianne and Margaret. Old Mr Dashwood liked his nephew, his nephew's wife, and their young daughters very much and for many years they all lived happily together at Norland Park.

Old Mr Dashwood died and Henry and his family read his will. They were very surprised at what they read there. Only a few years before his death, old Mr Dashwood had changed the words of his will.

John Dashwood, Henry's son, was about twenty-seven years old and he was rich. He had inherited money from his mother and he had also married a rich woman. John and his wife, Fanny, had one child – a boy called Harry. Harry was now four years old. Little Harry had often visited Norland Park with his parents and old Mr Dashwood had become so fond of[11] the young child that he had changed his will. The will said that while Henry Dashwood lived, he was the old man's heir, and Henry and his family could live at Norland Park. But the will also said that when Henry died, his wife and his three daughters would not inherit the property. Instead, the house and the land would belong to little Harry Dashwood – John Dashwood's son. Henry's second wife and his three daughters would have nothing.

'Do not worry, my dear,' Henry said to his wife after old Mr Dashwood's funeral[12]. 'Norland Park is our home now and I hope that it will be for many years. Our daughters will get married one day and they will look after us. We will all have many happy years here together.'

However, a year after old Mr Dashwood's death, Henry himself became very ill. When he knew that he was dying, he sent for his son, John. John Dashwood came to Norland Park immediately and stood by his father's bed.

'My dear John, you must look after your sisters and their mother,' Henry Dashwood said. 'Please promise me that you will do this. Your stepmother[13] and her girls will not have much money. When I am dead, Norland Park will belong to your son. But he is a very young child. You will be looking after everything. Promise me that you will help my dear wife and daughters.'

John Dashwood was not an unkind young man, but he was very careful with money.

'Yes, father,' John said. 'I promise that I will look after them.'

A few days later Henry Dashwood died and, very soon, everything changed. As soon as Henry's funeral had taken place, Fanny Dashwood, John Dashwood's wife, arrived at Norland Park. Little Harry and all her servants were with her. The house was Fanny's home now and she wanted to make sure that Mrs Dashwood and her girls understood this.

Fanny Dashwood was a cold and very selfish woman. She

had no kind feelings and she only thought of herself. She did not care about Mrs Dashwood and her daughters, but she was polite to them at first.

'You must all stay at Norland Park for as long as you wish,' Fanny told them. 'John and I will make changes, of course. But you will always be welcome guests here.'

Mrs Dashwood was now a guest in her own home and she was very unhappy. She had very little money and she was dependent[14] on John and Fanny. Fanny now gave orders to the servants and she decided how much money was spent. Mrs Dashwood had never liked Fanny, and she did not want to live at Norland Park any longer. But her eldest daughter, Elinor, persuaded[15] her to stay.

'John is our brother, mama[16],' Elinor said. 'We do not know him very well. We should spend some time with him. It will be better to stay here for a few months. Later, we can find a smaller house to live in, and remain friends with[17] John too.'

Elinor Dashwood had a pretty face and a fine figure. She was a kind and sensible girl. She always thought about things carefully. She had strong feelings, but she had good sense too. She had learnt to control her feelings.

Marianne, Elinor's younger sister, was clever, interesting and beautiful. She felt very strongly about everything and her feelings were always clear to everyone. Sensibility was more important than good sense to Marianne. Marianne was either very happy or completely miserable.

Mrs Dashwood behaved in the same way as her daughter, Marianne. She could not hide her feelings easily. Both Marianne and Mrs Dashwood were now very miserable. They could not believe that they would ever be happy again.

Mrs Dashwood's third daughter was named Margaret and she was aged thirteen. Margaret was more like sixteen-year-old Marianne than nineteen-year-old Elinor. Margaret was lively and independent. She did not like to be told what to do and she always said what she thought.

John Dashwood had been thinking carefully about his promise to his father. He decided to give each of his sisters £1000. But his wife, Fanny, did not agree with this decision. Fanny had always been rich, but she was very mean. She hated giving money away.

'Three thousand pounds!' Fanny cried. 'That money belongs to our dear little Harry. How can you be so unkind to your own son?'

'But I must so something to help my stepmother and my sisters,' John Dashwood replied. 'I made a promise to my father when he was dying. I promised that I would look after them. But you are right, Fanny. Perhaps £3000 is too much. The girls may marry well and have rich husbands. Then they will not need the money at all. £500 each will be more than enough, I am sure.'

'Certainly it will be enough,' Fanny said. 'If our Harry has many children of his own, he might need all his money. Also, there is an arrangement with your stepmother's family. When their mother dies, the girls will each have £3000. I have a better idea. Give Mrs Dashwood and her girls a gift of £50 from time to time. Find them a little house where they can all live very cheaply[18]. This way we shall all be happy.'

John Dashwood was delighted with Fanny's idea. It would save him a great deal of money and keep Fanny happy too.

'You are right, my dear,' John said to his wife. 'That is an excellent suggestion. £50 will be more than enough. My stepmother has a little money of her own. She already has everything that they need for their new home. She has china, linen[19] and a few pieces of furniture from Norland. The girls will not need any money at all!'

Mrs Dashwood and her daughters stayed on at Norland Park for nearly six months after Henry Dashwood's death. During this time, Fanny was often unkind and thoughtless and she upset Mrs Dashwood many times. But Mrs Dashwood enjoyed looking at other houses for her family to live in. There were several houses in the neighbourhood[20] that she liked, but Elinor persuaded her mother that they were all too big and expensive.

Fanny Dashwood had two brothers. Their names were Edward and Robert Ferrars. Twenty-four-year-old Edward Ferrars, Fanny's elder brother, now came to stay at Norland Park. He remained there for several weeks.

Edward Ferrars was not handsome, but he had a pleasant face and very good manners. Edward was very shy – he was uncomfortable when he talked with strangers or large groups of people, and he did not say much. But he was kind and thoughtful. He was very unlike his sister, Fanny.

Edward was always polite to Mrs Dashwood and her daughters. He felt sorry for them. He understood their feelings. Norland Park had been their home for many years. But it did not belong to them now and this was difficult for them.

Elinor and Edward were often together. They walked in the gardens, rode horses in the park, and sat next to each other every evening. Edward was not shy with Elinor and he always had something to say to her. Mrs Dashwood was sure that they were falling in love. She was delighted and she spoke to Marianne about it.

'I think that Edward loves our dear Elinor, and that she loves him too!' Mrs Dashwood told Marianne. 'If all goes well, your sister will be married in a few months and she will have a home of her own. I shall miss her very much. But Edward will make her happy, I am sure.'

Marianne shook her head and said, 'I am not sure about Edward, mama. He is very pleasant, but he is too quiet. He

'I think that Edward loves our dear Elinor, and that she loves him too!' said Mrs Dashwood.

never says anything that is interesting or exciting. He does not like music or poetry, and he does not understand art at all. But I suppose that he might be suitable for Elinor. She is quiet and sensible too. And she is easily pleased.

'I am very different from Elinor, mama,' Marianne went on. 'The man whom I marry must be lively, handsome and charming[21]. He must love art, poetry and music. He must have good manners and make me laugh. He must be able to speak well about interesting things. He must be perfect and please me in every way.'

Marianne sighed[22]. 'I do not think that I shall ever meet a man whom I can truly love,' she added sadly.

Mrs Dashwood laughed at her daughter's words. 'Marianne, you are not seventeen yet,' she said. 'There is plenty of time for you to find the perfect man!'

Marianne smiled and went to talk to her sister about Edward Ferrars.

'It is a pity[23] that Edward does not share[24] your love of art, Elinor,' Marianne began. 'You draw and paint so well, but Edward has very little interest in your work.'

'That is not true,' Elinor answered quickly. 'I have often spoken to Edward about art. His taste and opinions[25] are those of a real gentleman[26]. He does not say much when many people are listening, because he is shy. But he talks to me. I like him very much, Marianne.'

'You *like* him!' Marianne repeated. 'You are cold-hearted, Elinor! Where are your feelings of *love* for Edward Ferrars? Does he not love you?'

'I hope that Edward loves me,' Elinor replied quietly, 'but I cannot be sure. He has no profession[27] and very little money of his own. No one can live without money. Edward and his brother are dependent on their mother. Mrs Ferrars will expect her sons to choose rich women when they fall in love.'

'If Edward loves you and he is sensible, he will choose you. He will not care about money!' Marianne cried. 'Mama and I hope that you will soon be engaged. Then I shall love Edward as a brother!'

Elinor did not answer. She had noticed that Edward often looked unhappy. Perhaps there was something that he was hiding from her. Did Edward Ferrars have a secret? Elinor did not know. Although she was very fond of Edward, Elinor could not be completely sure of his true feelings for her.

Fanny Dashwood had noticed the friendship between her brother and Elinor, and it did not please her at all. Elinor Dashwood had very little money and Fanny thought that she was unsuitable in every way. Fanny believed that Elinor was not good enough for her brother. Fanny wanted to make Mrs Dashwood understand this.

'If my brothers behave well and do not upset our mother, they will both be rich men,' Fanny said. 'My mother expects Edward and Robert to marry suitable young women. I am sure that you understand me, Mrs Dashwood. My mother will be very angry if my brothers are tricked into unsuitable marriages.'

Mrs Dashwood was very upset by these words, but she was too angry to answer. She understood Fanny very well. Fanny was saying that Elinor was too poor to marry Edward Ferrars and she must not make him love her.

'We must leave Norland Park at once!' Mrs Dashwood told her daughters. 'We must find a home of our own. I will not live in the same house as Fanny Dashwood any longer!'

A few days later, Mrs Dashwood received a letter from one of her relations – a wealthy gentleman who lived at Barton Park, in Devon. The gentleman's name was Sir John Middleton and he owned a lot of land and property. Barton Cottage, one of the little houses on his land, was empty. Sir

John suggested that Mrs Dashwood and her daughters could rent[28] the cottage and live there.

Sir John's letter was so kind and friendly that Mrs Dashwood decided to move to Devon at once. After Fanny's unkind words, Mrs Dashwood wanted to live as far away from Norland Park as possible. Elinor agreed with her mother, and they sent a letter to Sir John the same day.

John Dashwood was a little embarrassed when he heard this news. His stepmother and sisters were going to live far away because of Fanny's behaviour. He offered to pay the rent for the first six months himself. Mrs Dashwood was delighted. She decided to rent Barton Cottage for a year.

'Our new home is called Barton Cottage,' she told all her friends and neighbours. 'It is in the county of Devon, about four miles north of the town of Exeter.'

Edward Ferrars looked very sad when he heard the news. 'Devon!' he said. 'That is so far away.'

Mrs Dashwood smiled at the young man kindly. 'Barton Cottage is not large,' she said. 'But our friends will always be welcome to stay there.'

The cottage already had some furniture in it. The Dashwoods were taking with them some china and a few pieces of furniture from Norland, their books, Marianne's piano and Elinor's pictures. The lives of Mrs Dashwood and her daughters would now be completely different. They were going to live simply, in a much smaller house. Mrs Dashwood sold her husband's carriage and horses, because she did not have enough money to keep them. There were very many servants at Norland Park, but she would only need three at Barton Cottage. As soon as the arrangements were made, three servants went to Devon. They were going to clean the cottage before the Dashwoods arrived.

'Dear, dear Norland, how sad I am to leave you!' Marianne said on their last evening in Norland Park. 'I love every room in this wonderful house! Every tree in the park is beautiful. Shall I ever be happy again?'

2

Barton

It was now September and the weather was fine. The journey from Sussex to Devon was a very long one. The Dashwoods had to travel for many hours in a carriage before they reached their new home. At first, the family felt miserable. But as they got nearer to Barton, they became happier. Devon was a beautiful county and the Dashwoods saw interesting views as they looked out of the carriage windows. There were narrow roads, and steep hills covered with trees. The land in this county was completely different from Sussex.

Barton Cottage was a small, well-built and comfortable little house. It stood beside a road in a valley. The village of Barton was on one of the hills behind the cottage. In front of the cottage, there was a lawn of green grass. A fence with a small wooden gate separated the lawn from the road. At the back of the cottage, there was a pretty garden surrounded by a wall.

Mrs Dashwood opened the small wooden gate and walked up to the front door of the cottage. Soon the family were standing in the sitting-room and looking around happily.

'Well, here we are, my dears,' Mrs Dashwood said to her three daughters. 'Our new home is not large, but we can have extra rooms built very easily. Marianne's piano looks very fine by the window. Now we must unpack our books and your paintings, Elinor. Then Barton Cottage will start to look like our own home.'

The three girls and their mother began to unpack their things at once. And the next day, just after breakfast, they had their first visitor – Sir John Middleton of Barton Park.

Sir John was a forty-year-old, good-looking, very friendly gentleman. Two servants came in his carriage with him. They brought fruit, vegetables and other food for Sir John's cousins. Sir John also brought a polite message from his wife, Lady Middleton. Mrs Dashwood was delighted. She invited the Middletons to visit Barton Cottage and they both called the next day.

Lady Middleton was tall, well-dressed and good-looking. She was about thirteen years younger than her husband. She was not very clever or well-educated, and she did not have much to say. But as she had brought one of her young sons with her, all the ladies talked about him.

Before the Middletons left the cottage, Sir John invited the Dashwoods to dinner at Barton Park.

'We both love having visitors,' he said. 'Our house is not far – just half a mile through the park. It is a very pleasant walk.'

Barton Park was a large, well-furnished house and the Middletons both enjoyed inviting young people to stay there. Sir John was a sportsman and he often went hunting and shooting with his friends. Lady Middleton spent most of her time with her children, but she enjoyed entertaining her neighbours too.

The Middletons were delighted with the Dashwoods. The three girls were charming and pretty and their mother was a very pleasant friend. Sir John was waiting to greet them when they arrived.

'Welcome! Welcome to Barton Park,' he said, laughing happily. 'I am afraid that we do not have many other guests here to meet you today. But my wife's mother, Mrs Jennings, has just arrived. And my good friend, Colonel Brandon, is staying with us. He lives at Delaford, which is not far away. So he is your neighbour, as well as mine.'

Mrs Jennings, Lady Middleton's mother, was a cheerful, fat old lady. Her two daughters had both married rich men. Her elder daughter was married to Sir John. Her younger daughter, Charlotte, had married a member of Parliament[29] named Thomas Palmer. Now Mrs Jennings' main interest was to find good husbands for all the unmarried ladies in the neighbourhood. Mrs Jennings was a kind woman but her manners were not always good. She loved to gossip. She found out other peoples' secrets and private business, and she talked about them.

At dinner, she sat between Elinor and Marianne.

'Well, my dears, you must tell me all about yourselves,' she said. 'I am sure that you both left young men in Sussex who were fond of you. They must have been sorry when you went away. But they will be coming to Barton soon, I am sure!'

Elinor smiled politely and Marianne shook her head. Neither sister answered the old lady, so she laughed and teased[30] them.

'I shall find out your secrets very soon, Miss Dashwood and Miss Marianne,' she said.

Colonel Brandon was a quiet, sensible man and he said very little. He was tall, with a serious face and good manners. The Colonel was about thirty-five years old and, as Mrs Jennings soon told the Dashwood girls, he was not married. Marianne and Margaret thought that he was too old to be interesting.

After dinner, Mrs Jennings continued to tease the Dashwood sisters. She made jokes about love and lovers. Lady Middleton looked bored with the conversation and said nothing. She only smiled when her four noisy children ran into the room and began to shout loudly.

Later in the evening, Sir John asked Marianne to play the piano and sing. Everyone praised[31] the young woman's singing, but only Colonel Brandon listened carefully and with real pleasure. Mrs Jennings noticed this and she was soon teasing the Colonel and Marianne too.

'Miss Marianne,' she said. 'Colonel Brandon has fallen in love with you. You sing and play delightfully. The Colonel is rich and you are beautiful. It will be an excellent marriage.'

Colonel Brandon did not care when Mrs Jennings teased him, but Marianne did not know if she should laugh or cry. She thought that the old lady was being very foolish.

'Colonel Brandon is far too old to fall in love,' Marianne told her family when they were home again. 'He said that he had a pain in his shoulder, so he was going to wear a thick, warm coat. Did you hear him say that? Men of his age should not marry – unless they need a nurse!'

'The Colonel is not old and he looks very healthy,' Elinor said with a smile. 'He does not need a nurse.'

Marianne did not reply. She was not interested in Colonel Brandon. Later, she spoke to her mother alone.

'Mama, I am worried about Edward Ferrars,' she said. 'Do you think that he is ill? We have been at Barton for nearly two weeks now. Edward knows that we are here. Why has he not come to see Elinor? And why will Elinor not talk about him? Elinor and Edward are so cold-hearted! I could not hide my feelings as Elinor does.'

The Dashwoods were very happy in their new home. They often visited the Middletons, and received calls from them. But because the Dashwoods had no carriage of their own, they did not travel far in the county. They met very few other people.

While the weather was fine, the girls went on long walks. Then there were several days of heavy rain. All the paths became wet and muddy and the girls had to stay at home.

Then, one morning, Marianne looked out of the sitting-room window and saw that the rain-clouds had disappeared. The sky was now blue and the sun was shining.

'Look, the sun is shining at last,' she said. 'Let us all go out for a walk!'

Elinor was drawing and Mrs Dashwood was reading, and they did not want to go out. Only Margaret wanted to go walking with her sister. Soon the two girls were walking up the nearest hill.

In the next valley, there was a fine old house called Allenham Court. Marianne and Margaret stood on the top of the hill and admired[32] the property. Sir John had told them that the house belonged to an old lady whose name was Mrs Smith. She was too ill to call on people and she did not have many visitors.

'What exciting weather!' Marianne cried as the wind blew in their faces. 'I could walk here for a long time without getting tired!'

The girls walked on, laughing and talking. Suddenly, the rain-clouds returned and the sky became dark. Soon rain began to fall heavily.

There were no trees or buildings nearby. There was nowhere for the sisters to shelter[33] from the rain. They turned back at once to go home. They ran as fast as they could, down the hill and back towards the cottage. Soon, they were both very wet.

At first, Marianne was in front, but then she slipped on the wet grass and fell to the ground. She cried out in pain. Margaret was running too fast and she could not stop. The young girl ran down to the cottage and reached the garden safely. But poor Marianne had hurt her ankle and she could not move. She lay on the grass, getting wetter and wetter in the cold rain.

'Margaret, I cannot stand!' Marianne shouted. 'Bring someone to help me!'

At that moment, a young man came over the hill. He was carrying a gun and had his two hunting dogs with him. When he saw Marianne, he put down his gun and ran to help her. Marianne tried to get up, but her ankle hurt her too much.

Without speaking, the gentleman lifted Marianne in his arms and carried her down the hill. He quickly reached the house and took her inside.

The Dashwoods were very surprised to see Marianne in the arms of a strange young man. They watched in silence as he carried Marianne into the sitting-room and placed her carefully on a chair.

'I surprised you, and I apologise,' the young gentleman said politely. 'But this lady needed my help. She has hurt her ankle and she cannot walk alone. And, as you see, she is very wet and cold.'

'Please, do not apologise,' Mrs Dashwood replied. 'It is lucky that you were nearby. Please sit down. May I ask your name, sir?'

The young man was extremely handsome and his voice and manners were very pleasing.

'My name is Willoughby,' he said and he bowed[34] politely towards Mrs Dashwood. 'I am, at present, living at Allenham. I must not sit down because my clothes are wet. Perhaps I may call tomorrow? I would like to ask about the young lady's health.'

'You will be very welcome,' Mrs Dashwood replied. 'The lady whom you rescued[35] is my daughter, Miss Marianne Dashwood. These are her sisters, Elinor and Margaret. We are all very grateful to you.'

The young man bowed again and left the room without saying another word.

The Dashwoods were very surprised to see Marianne in the arms of a strange young man.

The Dashwoods all looked at each other.

'What a handsome young man!' Margaret cried. 'I look forward to seeing him again! What do you think of him, Marianne?'

Marianne smiled, but she could not speak.

Willoughby! His name was Willoughby! Here at last was the perfect young man of her dreams!

When Sir John Middleton called at Barton Cottage, Mrs Dashwood told him about Marianne's fall and her handsome rescuer, Willoughby.

'John Willoughby?' Sir John cried, laughing happily. 'Is he in the neighbourhood? What good news! I shall invite him to dinner on Thursday.'

'Do you know him?' Mrs Dashwood asked. 'What kind of young man is he?'

'Willoughby is a fine young man,' Sir John replied. 'He stays in Devon every year. He has many fine horses and he rides very well. He shoots well too.'

'Does he have property near here?' Elinor asked. 'He said that he was staying at Allenham.'

'Mrs Smith – the old lady at Allenham Court – is his aunt,' Sir John explained to Elinor. 'Willoughby is Mrs Smith's heir. He has a house in the county of Somerset too. He would make a fine husband for any girl. Mr Willoughby is certainly worth catching, Miss Dashwood.' Then he added with a laugh, 'Miss Marianne has already caught Colonel Brandon, remember.'

'Sir John, my daughters do not "catch" young men,' Mrs Dashwood said, smiling. 'But if Willoughby is a suitable neighbour, we shall all be glad to meet him at Barton Park.'

'He is a very lively young man,' Sir John answered. 'On Christmas Day last year he came to our party. He danced all the evening, and then he got up early the next morning to go hunting!'

'Oh! He is just the kind of man that I like!' Marianne cried, her eyes shining with happiness. 'I very much want to see Mr Willoughby again.'

3

Marianne and Willoughby

Marianne soon had her wish. Willoughby called early the next morning and he was warmly welcomed by Mrs Dashwood. Willoughby himself was delighted by the Dashwoods and everyone soon noticed that he admired Marianne Dashwood.

Elinor Dashwood had a pretty face and a fine figure. But her younger sister, Marianne, was beautiful. Marianne had dark shining eyes and she loved to talk about her ideas and feelings. She and Willoughby both liked art, literature, music and dancing. Willoughby admired the same poets who Marianne loved. Marianne was delighted.

Willoughby visited Barton Cottage every day. For a few days after her fall, Marianne could not walk, so she could not leave the house. But she did not care. All she thought about was Willoughby.

The two young people talked together. They sang their favourite songs together. After only a few days, the beautiful young woman and her handsome rescuer had told each other their ideas on every subject. Marianne was completely happy for the first time in her life. Willoughby was perfect in every way!

Elinor was a little unhappy about her sister's behaviour. As usual, Marianne thought only of her feelings. Elinor knew that sensibility was more important to Marianne than good sense. Marianne thought that Willoughby loved her and so she believed it.

Mrs Dashwood was happy too. She did not agree with Elinor. Mrs Dashwood was hoping that her second daughter would soon be engaged. She wanted Marianne to marry their charming, handsome neighbour.

Elinor saw that Colonel Brandon also admired Marianne. Elinor felt sorry for the Colonel. She was angry when Willoughby and Marianne laughed at the older man who was so different from themselves.

'Everyone speaks well of Brandon, but no one cares about him,' Willoughby said one day. 'We are all delighted to see him, but no one wants to talk to him.'

'That is exactly what I think,' Marianne said.

'You are both being unkind about Colonel Brandon,' Elinor said quickly. 'His neighbours admire him and I enjoy talking to him.'

'Lady Middleton and Mrs Jennings admire him,' Willoughby said with a careless laugh. 'But no one thinks that their opinions are important.'

'The Colonel has good sense,' Elinor replied. 'And I think that he has a kind heart.'

'Perhaps he does have a kind heart. But what about his feelings?' Marianne asked. 'You think that the Colonel is sensible. Willoughby and I think that he is very dull[36]!'

The month of October passed very happily for Marianne. She thought about nothing but her love for Willoughby. They met at every dance and party in the neighbourhood. They did not try to hide their feelings for each other. Mrs Jennings teased them and made many jokes about love, but Marianne and Willoughby did not care.

Elinor was not as happy as her sister. She often thought about Norland Park and how her friendship with Edward

Ferrars had started there. Elinor had hoped to see Edward again, but he did not come to Barton.

Elinor enjoyed sensible conversations and she liked to talk to Colonel Brandon. Elinor was not in love with the Colonel, but she enjoyed being with him. Whenever the Middletons invited guests to Barton Park, Elinor always met Colonel Brandon there. There was often music and dancing, but Elinor and the Colonel usually talked.

They were sitting together one evening when Brandon said, 'Your sister does not believe that anyone can love more than once.' Then he looked sadly at Marianne and Willoughby, who were dancing together.

'My sister is very young and she feels strongly about her ideas,' Elinor replied. 'When she is older, perhaps her feelings may change.'

Brandon thought for a moment and then he said quietly, 'I used to know a lady who was very like your sister. Her ideas and feelings were very much like your sister's ideas and feelings. The young lady believed that only happiness and love were important. But she was unlucky and later, her ideas changed. I ... '

The Colonel stopped speaking and said nothing more on the subject. Elinor was sure that he was remembering a woman whom he had loved. But she did not ask him any questions.

The next day, Marianne came to tell Elinor some surprising news. Her eyes were shining with excitement.

'You will not guess what has happened!' she said. 'Willoughby is giving me a horse! His servant is bringing it from Somerset tomorrow. Willoughby says that the horse will suit me perfectly. The horse's name is Queen Mab. I shall enjoy riding on the hills with Willoughby!'

'Marianne!' Elinor said. 'You cannot accept an expensive

gift like that from Willoughby! It would be completely wrong. Also, we have nowhere to keep the animal and we do not have enough money to look after it. You must tell Willoughby that you cannot accept his gift.'

Marianne was upset at first, but at last she decided that her sister was right. Sadly, she spoke to Willoughby about it the next day.

'Then I shall keep the horse until you can use it,' Willoughby said. 'When you have your own home, Queen Mab will be there waiting for you.'

Elinor was nearby and she heard this conversation. She was very surprised. Men only gave expensive gifts to ladies if they were engaged to them. Elinor now believed that Willoughby and Marianne must be engaged.

Later in the afternoon, Margaret told Elinor something that made Marianne and Willoughby's engagement even more certain.

'Oh, Elinor! I have a secret to tell you about Marianne,' Margaret said excitedly. 'I am sure that she will be married very soon. Willoughby has a lock[37] of Marianne's hair!'

'Are you sure, Margaret?' Elinor asked. She was worried by her sister's words.

'Oh, yes, I am quite sure,' Margaret replied. 'Willoughby and Marianne were in the sitting-room together. I saw Willoughby pick up a pair of scissors. He was talking to Marianne and laughing. Then he cut off a lock of her hair. Marianne's face became very red, but she laughed too. Then Willoughby kissed the lock of hair and put it in his pocket!'

Elinor believed what Margaret had told her. Elinor was becoming very worried about Marianne's behaviour, but she said nothing to their mother about it.

One evening in October, the Dashwoods went to Barton Park for dinner with Sir John and Lady Middleton. Mrs

Jennings and Colonel Brandon were also there. Mrs Jennings spoke to Elinor and Margaret about love and lovers. She was quite sure that Marianne and Willoughby would soon be married. The old lady now wanted to know if Elinor was in love too.

'Tell me the name of the young man who is in love with Elinor,' Mrs Jennings said to Margaret. 'I am sure that you know his name.'

'Yes, I do,' Margaret replied. 'But I cannot tell you, can I, Elinor?'

Mrs Dashwood and Margaret laughed and Elinor tried to laugh too. But she looked unhappy and Marianne felt sorry for her.

'Please do not talk about this, Margaret,' Marianne said.

'You told me his name yourself, Marianne,' Margaret said quickly.

'Oh! Then you can tell us the gentleman's name, Margaret,' Mrs Jennings said.

'His name begins with F,' Margaret answered with a laugh. 'That is all that I can say.'

Mrs Jennings was ready with more questions, but Lady Middleton began to talk about the weather.

Colonel Brandon saw that Elinor was embarrassed and he tried to help her. He persuaded Marianne to sing for them, and she sat down at the piano and began to play. Willoughby walked quickly across the room and stood beside her.

No one said anything more about Edward Ferrars and Elinor felt much happier.

A few minutes later, Sir John and his guests talked about spending a day together. They made a plan to visit Whitwell, a very large fine house about twelve miles from Barton Park. The house belonged to Colonel Brandon's brother-in-law[38], who was presently abroad, on holiday.

Colonel Brandon agreed to take Sir John and his friends

to Whitwell. Everyone would be able to go into the beautiful house, and see its fine pictures and furniture. There was also a large park around the house, with a lake. People could ride or walk round the park, and they could sail on the lake in boats. Then everyone would sit in the pretty garden and eat a delicious meal.

On the day of the visit to Whitwell, everyone was excited. They all met at Barton Park early in the morning. First, they would have breakfast. Then at ten o'clock, they would all start the journey to the house of Brandon's brother-in-law.

During breakfast, a servant arrived with the post. There were several letters for Sir John and one for Colonel Brandon. The Colonel looked at the address on his letter and recognised the writing. Then he stood up quickly and left the room.

'What is the matter with Brandon?' Sir John asked, but no one could tell him.

The Colonel himself returned after about five minutes. He looked very worried.

'You have not had bad news, I hope?' Mrs Jennings asked him quickly.

'No, thank you, ma'am. I have some important business, that is all.'

'Business, Colonel?' Mrs Jennings repeated with a laugh. 'I think that I understand your *business*. How is she, Colonel?'

The old lady laughed again, but Brandon did not answer her. Looking very unhappy, he turned to speak to Lady Middleton.

'I am very sorry, ma'am, but I have to leave,' he said. 'I must go to London at once. I am afraid that you cannot go to Whitwell without me. The visit cannot take place now.'

'Start your journey to London tomorrow, Brandon!' Sir John cried. 'You cannot disappoint all your friends now!'

'I am very sorry, ma'am, but I have to leave. The visit to Whitwell cannot take place now.'

'I am sorry, that is not possible,' Colonel Brandon replied. 'I must go today.'

'Then come back quickly,' Lady Middleton told him. 'We will visit Whitwell another day very soon.'

'I shall not be coming back to Barton for some time,' the Colonel told her. He turned to speak to Elinor.

'Can I hope to see you and your sister in London this winter, Miss Dashwood?' he asked her quietly.

'I am afraid that you will not, Colonel,' Elinor replied.

The Colonel looked disappointed, but he said nothing. He then bowed to Marianne and left the room with Sir John.

Everyone began talking at once. They were all very angry with Colonel Brandon. They were disappointed too.

'The Colonel's business is with Miss Williams, I am sure,' Mrs Jennings said quietly.

'Who is Miss Williams?' Marianne asked.

Mrs Jennings smiled. She enjoyed gossiping with her friends. The old lady whispered to Elinor.

'She is a relation of the Colonel's – a very close relation,' she replied. 'Miss Eliza Williams is his daughter. Everyone knows about her.'

At that moment, Sir John came back into the room and everyone stopped talking.

'Well, Brandon has left, but we must not waste the day,' Sir John said cheerfully. 'The carriages are here and the weather is fine. Let us all spend the day driving about on the hills. We can come back here to Barton Park for dinner. And, after dinner, there will be a dance!'

Everyone was very happy with this suggestion. They all stood up, laughing and smiling, and went outside. In front of the house, carriages were waiting to take Sir John and his friends to the hills. But two people did not join the others for the day. Willoughby got into his curricle[39] and Marianne climbed up onto the seat beside him. Then the young man turned the two black horses and drove the yellow carriage away at great speed.

At dinner that evening, Willoughby sat between Elinor and Marianne. Mrs Jennings sat opposite them. The old lady began to speak to Marianne.

'I know where you and Willoughby spent the day, Miss Marianne!' Mrs Jennings said loudly. 'I hope that you like the house that you will live in one day. Allenham Court is a fine place, is it not? I hope that I shall be invited there very soon!'

Marianne's face became very red and she did not answer.

When they were home again, Elinor spoke to Marianne alone.

'Your behaviour today was wrong,' Elinor said. 'You should not have gone to Allenham Court. Old Mrs Smith did not invite you, I am sure. Willoughby was wrong too. He should not have taken you there. Allenham is not his home or yours, though it may be one day.'

Marianne looked away and her eyes filled with tears.

'Perhaps I should not have gone to Allenham,' she said. 'But Willoughby wanted me to see the house and I agreed to go with him. I wanted to.

'Oh, Elinor, Allenham is a beautiful house. There is a very pretty sitting-room upstairs, with a lovely view of the hills from its windows. Willoughby says that if £200 were spent on modern furniture, the room would be perfect!'

4

Two Young Men

A few days passed, but Willoughby and Marianne said nothing about their engagement. Elinor could not understand it. Willoughby visited Barton Cottage every day and he spent most of his time with Marianne. The two young people were completely happy. Willoughby's love for the beautiful girl and his liking for all her family became stronger as each day passed.

One evening, Mrs Dashwood was talking about her plans to change Barton Cottage. The Dashwoods wanted to build extra rooms in the cottage and decorate it with new paint.

'Oh, do not change anything in the cottage, my dear Mrs Dashwood!' Willoughby cried. 'Nothing must be changed! Barton Cottage is perfect!'

'But the stairs are too narrow and the fireplace in the kitchen needs to be repaired,' Elinor said with a smile.

'Change nothing in this dear little house,' Willoughby repeated. 'And never, never change your feelings towards me. We have all been so happy here. Everything must stay the same. Please promise me that nothing will be changed.'

Mrs Dashwood smiled at Willoughby's words and a few hours later, Willoughby got ready to return to Allenham.

'We must call on Lady Middleton tomorrow morning,' Mrs Dashwood told him. 'But shall we see you here at dinner tomorrow evening?'

Willoughby bowed politely and said that he would be at the cottage at four o'clock.

The next morning, Mrs Dashwood, Elinor and Margaret went to visit Lady Middleton. Marianne stayed at home.

When the ladies returned, Willoughby's yellow curricle, with its two black horses, was outside the cottage.

The Dashwoods went inside. Moments later, they were surprised to see Marianne run past them. She was holding a handkerchief to her face. Weeping loudly, she ran upstairs to her room.

The door of the drawing-room was open and Willoughby was standing by the fireplace. His back was towards them.

'What is the matter with Marianne?' Mrs Dashwood cried. 'Is she ill?'

Willoughby turned around. He looked very unhappy.

'No, Marianne is not ill,' he replied. 'But I have had some very bad news and she is upset. Mrs Smith has given me her orders. I cannot disobey her. She is sending me on business to London. I must go at once.'

'But you will not be away for long, I hope?' Mrs Dashwood asked with a smile.

'You are very kind,' Willoughby answered, 'but I am afraid that I cannot give you an answer. I never visit Mrs Smith more than once a year. I shall not be returning to Allenham Court for some time.'

'But what about your friends here at Barton Cottage? You are welcome to visit us at any time, you know that.'

Willoughby could not look at Mrs Dashwood. His face became very red.

'You are very kind,' he said again, quietly. 'But I have many things to do in London. I cannot promise that I will return soon. I must go now. There is no more to say. I must leave you at once.'

Willoughby bowed and left the room quickly. In a few minutes, he was out of the house, in his carriage, and driving away.

Mrs Dashwood and Elinor looked at each other. They did not know what to think. Had Willoughby and Marianne quarrelled[40]? What about their engagement? Were they engaged at all?

Mrs Dashwood did not want to have a bad opinion of Willoughby. She wanted to believe that there was a very important reason for his strange behaviour. She thought that the young man loved her daughter.

'It cannot be Willoughby's fault[41] that he has to go to London,' Mrs Dashwood said to Elinor. 'Mrs Smith must have heard about his friendship with Marianne. It has made the old lady angry. Perhaps Willoughby cannot tell his aunt about his engagement to Marianne at this time. Perhaps he thinks that he must leave Devon for a short time. Do you agree with me, Elinor?'

'I do not know. We cannot be sure, mama,' Elinor replied.

'Not sure?' Mrs Dashwood cried. 'Have you no feelings, Elinor? Everyone can see how much Willoughby and Marianne love each other!'

'I can believe in their love,' Elinor said, 'but I cannot believe in their engagement. Neither Willoughby nor Marianne have spoken about their engagement. Why not? Why must it be a secret?'

'I am sure that Mrs Smith is the problem,' Mrs Dashwood said quickly. 'Willoughby must be very careful. He is very dependent on his aunt. He will inherit her property when she dies. He was very upset. You saw that, Elinor. He did not want to leave Marianne.'

'I am very fond of Willoughby, mama. I shall say nothing more against him,' Elinor said. 'We will know the truth very soon.'

When Marianne came downstairs for dinner, her eyes were red. She had been weeping. She did not eat and she did not speak. After a few minutes, she began to cry again and she soon left the room.

That night, Elinor heard Marianne weeping and in the

morning, Marianne had a bad headache. She had been awake all night. She did not eat any breakfast. Instead, she went for a walk by herself. In the evening, she sang all of Willoughby's favourite songs and then she began to cry again. She wept for many hours.

After a few days, Marianne was a little calmer, but she was still very unhappy. No letters came from Willoughby.

'Mama, please ask Marianne about her engagement,' Elinor said to her mother.

'No, no, I cannot,' Mrs Dashwood said. 'Marianne will tell us all about it when she is ready. She is too unhappy to talk about it at the moment.'

About a week after Willoughby had left Devon, Marianne agreed to go for a walk with her sisters. When they stepped onto the road outside the cottage, they stopped for a moment. A gentleman was riding his horse towards them.

'It is him!' Marianne cried, 'It is Willoughby!'

'No, this gentleman is not tall enough,' Elinor said. 'It cannot be Willoughby.'

'It is Willoughby, it *is*. I knew that he would come,' Marianne said and she began to run towards the visitor.

But Marianne was disappointed. The visitor was not Willoughby – it was Edward Ferrars.

'He is here, at last!' Elinor thought.

Edward got off his horse and walked with the girls into Barton Cottage. He was very quiet and he looked unhappy. He did not look at Elinor.

'Have you come from London, Edward?' Marianne asked the young man.

'No, I have not come from London,' Edward replied. 'I have been in Devon for two weeks.'

'Two weeks!' Marianne repeated in surprise. 'Why have you not come to see us before today?'

Edward looked very embarrassed. 'I have been staying with friends near Plymouth,' he said quietly.

'Have you been in Sussex recently?' Elinor asked the young man.

'I was at Norland about a month ago,' Edward replied.

'Dear, dear Norland!' Marianne cried. 'I miss our beautiful home in Sussex. But Barton is beautiful, too, is it not? Look at those hills! And over there is Barton Park, surrounded by all its lovely trees!'

'Barton is certainly in a beautiful part of Devon,' Edward replied. 'But in winter, these roads must be very wet and muddy.'

Marianne felt sorry for a man who thought about mud rather than beautiful trees.

Elinor was pleased to see Edward, but she could not understand why he had come. He did not look happy to see her at all.

Mrs Dashwood gave Edward a warm welcome to Barton Cottage and invited him to stay for several days. Edward accepted her invitation and he began to be more cheerful.

'What are your plans, Edward?' Mrs Dashwood asked him at dinner. 'Have you decided on a profession? Will you join the army or the navy? Or will you study law? Will you become a famous soldier, sailor, or lawyer? Your mother has great plans for you, I am sure.'

Edward smiled and shook his head.

'I shall never be a great man,' he said. 'And I do not want to be famous. I am very shy, as you know, and I do not like meeting strangers.'

'But we are your friends, Edward,' Marianne said. 'You do not need to be shy with us. Do not hide your true feelings from us.'

'I apologise,' said Edward. 'I know that you are my friends and I shall try to be more cheerful.'

Elinor was sorry for her friend. He was certainly very unhappy, but she could not understand why.

At breakfast the next morning, Marianne saw that Edward was wearing a ring with a lock of hair in it.

'You are wearing a new ring, Edward,' Marianne said. 'Is that a lock of your sister's hair inside it? I thought that Fanny's hair was darker.'

Edward answered very quietly. 'You are right. This is my sister's hair,' he said. But he looked at Elinor as he spoke. She was sure that the lock of hair was her own. She felt pleased, but she did not say anything.

Later that morning, Sir John and Mrs Jennings came to visit. Mrs Jennings was very interested to hear that Edward's last name was Ferrars. She was already thinking of jokes about the letter F. She was already thinking of teasing Elinor about Edward.

Edward Ferrars stayed at Barton Cottage for a week. During that time, he became happier, but he said very little. Elinor believed that his mother was making Edward unhappy. But Mrs Dashwood had another idea.

'Edward,' she said as he was leaving. 'You have nothing to do. That is why you are not happy. You are an educated man. You should have a profession.'

'I agree, Mrs Dashwood,' Edward said sadly. 'I would like to be a clergyman, but my family do not believe that this is a good profession. My parents wanted me to be a soldier or a lawyer, but these professions were not right for me. When I was eighteen, my parents sent me to study in Oxford. However, since then, I have done nothing.

'And I believe that I will never do what I wish to do,' the young man added sadly.

'Dear Edward, try to be happy,' Mrs Dashwood said. 'The

'You are wearing a new ring, Edward,' Marianne said. 'Is that a lock of your sister's hair inside it?'

future may be better than you think.'

Edward bowed politely. He thanked Mrs Dashwood for her kindness. Then he smiled sadly at Elinor and left Barton Cottage without another word.

Marianne had wept when Willoughby went away. But when Edward left, Elinor did not show her feelings. She sat down at a little table in the sitting-room and began to draw. She was busy all day, but she was thinking of Edward. Elinor was very worried about him. Then she remembered the ring that Edward was wearing. He was wearing a ring with a lock of hair in it – hair which she believed was hers – and she felt much happier.

5

New Friends

One morning, about a week after Edward left Barton Cottage, Elinor was sitting at her little table again. She was drawing a picture and thinking of Edward. Suddenly, she heard the sound of the garden gate opening. She stood up and looked out of the window.

Five visitors were standing at the front door of the cottage – one of them was Sir John Middleton. He knocked on the window and Elinor opened it.

Sir John put his head in through the window and said, 'I have brought some strangers to see you. Tell me what you think of them!' And he laughed.

Before Elinor could reply, Mrs Jennings shouted through the window too.

'How are you, my dear?' the old lady cried cheerfully. 'I have brought my younger daughter, Charlotte, to see you.

Her husband, Mr Palmer, is here too.'

Elinor ran to the front door and opened it. Margaret and Mrs Dashwood had heard the voices, and immediately they came downstairs to welcome their visitors. Soon they were all drinking tea in the sitting-room.

Charlotte Palmer was very different from her elder sister, Lady Middleton. Charlotte was short, with a round pretty face. She talked and smiled all the time – except when she was laughing.

Mr Palmer bowed to the ladies and did not say anything. Then he sat down, picked up a newspaper, and began to read it.

'What a sweet place this is now, Mrs Dashwood!' said Charlotte. 'You have made this room so comfortable! And look at these pretty drawings! Are they yours, Miss Dashwood? How clever you are! Do you not agree, Mr Palmer?'

Mr Palmer went on reading his paper and did not say a word.

'We were so surprised when Charlotte and Thomas arrived last night,' Mrs Jennings said with a laugh. 'Charlotte should not have travelled. She is expecting a child[42] in February. But she is here, so you must all come to dinner tomorrow. Miss Marianne must come too.'

'Yes, you must come,' Sir John said. 'If the weather is bad, I will send my carriage for you.'

However, the following day, only Elinor and Marianne went to Barton Park. Mrs Dashwood and Margaret stayed at home.

As Marianne and Elinor walked into the drawing-room of Barton Park, Mrs Jennings greeted the sisters in her usual, cheerful way. Charlotte stood up, smiled happily, and ran across the room to speak to the Dashwood sisters.

'I am so glad that you have come today. Mr Palmer and I

'What a sweet place this is now, Mrs Dashwood!' said Charlotte.

have to leave tomorrow,' she said with a laugh. 'But we will all meet again in London. Very soon, I hope.'

'We are not going to London this winter,' Elinor said.

'You are not going to London!' Charlotte cried. 'But you must, Miss Dashwood!

'My dear Mr Palmer,' Charlotte said to her husband as he came into the room, 'you must persuade the Miss Dashwoods to go to London this winter. Willoughby is sure to be there,' she added, smiling at Marianne.

Mr Palmer did not answer. He looked out of the window and began to complain about the weather. It was now the month of November and cold winds were blowing.

Elinor and Charlotte went and sat near Mrs Jennings.

'Willoughby lives near you in Somerset, I believe,' Elinor said to Charlotte. 'Do you know him well?'

'Oh, very well, though I have never spoken to him. We have never met in Somerset, but I have seen him many times in London. Everyone there knows that your sister will marry Willoughby. Colonel Brandon told me this, when I saw him in London.'

'Are you sure?' Elinor asked in surprise.

'Well, my mother wrote and told me about your sister and Willoughby,' Charlotte said. 'So when I saw the Colonel, I asked him. He did not answer me immediately. But he believes that they will marry, I am sure.

'You believe this too, do you not, mama?' Charlotte said, looking at Mrs Jennings.

Elinor was very surprised by Charlotte's words and she wanted to hear more. 'Do you know Colonel Brandon well?' she asked.

'Oh, yes,' Charlotte said with a laugh. 'A few years ago, the Colonel wanted to marry me. But my mother decided that I must marry Mr Palmer and I am very happy with him.'

When he heard his name, Mr Palmer looked up from his

newspaper and frowned[43]. Mrs Jennings saw the frown on her son-in-law's face and laughed.

'Well, you can be angry now, Mr Palmer, but it is too late!' she cried. 'You married my Charlotte and you cannot give her back to me. We do not care about your frowns at all!'

The Palmers left Barton Park the next day, but the Middletons soon had some other visitors.

Mrs Jennings went to Exeter. While she was there, she met Anne and Lucy Steele, two young ladies who were her relations. Sir John invited them to Barton Park and they arrived a few days later.

The Miss Steeles were delighted to be at Barton Park and they were very polite to Sir John and Lady Middleton. The young ladies praised everything at Barton Park – the house, its furniture and, most of all, Lady Middleton's children. That, of course, pleased their parents very much.

Sir John talked excitedly about the new visitors when he saw the Dashwoods the next day.

'You must come and meet the Miss Steeles!' Sir John said. 'Lady Middleton says that they are the sweetest girls in the world! Lucy is so pretty and she is so kind to the children. She is always playing with them. Our visitors want to meet you, of course. You must come to Barton Park this week.'

Elinor and Marianne met Anne and Lucy Steele a few days later. Miss Steele was nearly thirty and she had a plain face. She talked a lot, but she had nothing interesting to say. Lucy Steele was about twenty-three. She had a pretty face and very bright, intelligent eyes. She looked carefully at each person that she spoke to, and smiled. Both girls said that they were delighted to meet Elinor and Marianne, but they were more interested in Lady Middleton's children.

Sir John and Lady Middleton had four children and they

all behaved very badly. They shouted loudly, they pulled the young ladies' hair and they threw the ladies' handkerchiefs out of the window.

'How sweet the little darlings are!' Miss Steele said with a laugh. 'How they love teasing us!'

As Miss Steele put her arms around Annamaria, her brooch scratched the little girl's arm. The three-year-old child screamed and screamed until her mother gave her some sweets and took her away.

'Lady Middleton is a very good mother!' Miss Steele cried.

Marianne said nothing, but Elinor agreed politely.

'I love the Middletons' children!' Lucy added. 'They are delightful. They are so clever and lively. Quiet children are so dull. Do you agree, Miss Dashwood?'

'When I am at Barton Park, I become very fond of dull, quiet children,' Elinor replied.

Lucy did not know how to reply to this.

Miss Steele spoke next.

'I am sure that you and your sister were sorry to leave Sussex, Miss Dashwood,' Anne Steele said with a smile. 'You must have known many handsome young men there. We cannot live without handsome young men, can we?'

Elinor was very surprised by these vulgar[44] words and Lucy looked unhappy. She frowned at her sister and said, 'I am sure that there are lots of young men in Barton, Anne.'

'Well, I hope so!' Miss Steele cried. 'But I think that the place is rather dull. Exeter is full of young men. There are too many, in fact. There's Mr Rose, Dr Simpson —'

'Please be quiet, Anne!' Lucy said sharply. 'Perhaps Miss Dashwood is not interested in young men. Or perhaps she does not want to talk about them,' she added. Then she looked at Elinor and smiled a sly[45] smile.

Elinor did not like this kind of conversation and she did not like the Miss Steeles either. Miss Steele was vulgar and stupid. Lucy was sly and did not say what she thought. Elinor did not want to be friends with them. She was pleased when she and Marianne were home again.

However, Sir John Middleton did not think the same thoughts as Elinor. He had other ideas about his young friends. He wanted the Miss Dashwoods and the Miss Steeles to like each other. He had soon told Anne and Lucy Steele all about the Dashwoods and their friends. He told the Miss Steeles that Marianne loved John Willoughby and that she was engaged to him.

Often when Elinor was at Barton Park, Mrs Jennings teased her about the letter F. Then one day, Sir John said, 'Elinor Dashwood is in love too. Her young man's name is Ferrars. But it is a secret, so please do not gossip about it.'

'Mr Ferrars!' Miss Steele cried. She turned to speak to Elinor. 'He is the brother of your sister-in-law, Fanny Dashwood, I believe. We know Mr Ferrars very well, Miss Dashwood. He often stays at our uncle's house, in Plymouth.'

Elinor was very surprised to hear this and she wanted to know more. But Lucy frowned at her sister and Anne stopped talking at once.

6

Lucy's Secret

Marianne Dashwood did not like the Steeles and she did not try to hide her feelings. Elinor did not like the Steeles either, but she did hide her feelings. She did not want to be rude to Sir John's visitors.

Lucy Steele's conversation was amusing and enjoyable – for a short time. But she was not well-educated and she did not have anything interesting to say. Also, she was not always honest – she did not always tell the truth. She flattered[46] the Middletons and she said that she was very fond of Elinor too.

Lucy very much wanted to be Elinor's friend. She was always trying to talk to Elinor alone. Elinor was soon tired of Lucy and her gossip.

One day, they were walking in the park together.

'Miss Dashwood, do you know Mrs Ferrars?' Lucy asked. 'She is the mother-in-law of your brother, John.' Then she added with a sly smile, 'I am sure that you think that is a strange question.'

'Well, yes, I do,' Elinor replied. 'I have never met Mrs Ferrars and I know nothing about her.'

'Oh dear, I am sorry!' Lucy cried. 'But one day soon, Mrs Ferrars will be very important to me. In fact, Miss Dashwood, I shall soon be part of her family!'

'What do you mean?' Elinor said in great surprise. 'Do you know her son, Robert Ferrars? Are you telling me that you are — ?'

'No. I am not talking about Mr Robert Ferrars,' Lucy replied, with another sly smile. 'I am talking about his elder brother, Mr Edward Ferrars. I am engaged to Edward Ferrars.'

Elinor was shocked. She did not know what to say.

'I have surprised you, Miss Dashwood,' Lucy went on. 'No one knows about our engagement. I know that you will keep this secret. I trust[47] you, and Mr Ferrars trusts you too. He thinks of you as a sister. He has often told me so.'

Elinor tried to hide her feelings, but it was very difficult.

'Have you and Edward Ferrars been engaged for a long time?' she asked quietly.

'We have been secretly engaged for four years.' Lucy replied. 'We met when Edward was studying with my uncle, Mr Pratt, who is a tutor[48] in Plymouth. Of course, Edward and

I were very young when we met. But Edward persuaded me to become engaged.'

Elinor did not know what to say next. She trusted Edward and she believed that he loved her. She was sure that he would never hurt her. Elinor did not trust Lucy and she did not believe that she was telling the truth.

'I think there is a mistake,' Elinor said at last. 'We cannot be talking about the same Mr Ferrars.'

'Oh, yes, we are!' Lucy cried. 'We are both talking about Mr Edward Ferrars, the eldest son of Mrs Ferrars of Park Street, London. He is the elder brother of your sister-in-law, Mrs John Dashwood. He is the man whom I love.'

'It is very strange,' Elinor said slowly. 'Edward has never spoken to me about you.'

'It is not strange at all,' Lucy replied. 'Our engagement has to be a secret. I do not know how long Edward and I must wait before we can get married. Who knows when we will be together?' Lucy sighed. 'But Edward has given me his picture,' she said. 'Look, here it is. I always carry it with me.'

Lucy took a small picture out of her pocket and showed it to Elinor. It was a painting of the face of Edward Ferrars. Elinor looked at the picture sadly.

'I shall keep your secret, Lucy,' Elinor said quietly. 'But why are you telling me about it?'

'I cannot talk to anyone else about this,' Lucy replied. 'Anne knows, of course, but she is not much help to me. I have been so unhappy for the last four years! Sometimes, I want to end our engagement. But that would upset my dear Edward too much. What would you do, Miss Dashwood?'

As she spoke, Lucy Steele put Edward's picture back in her pocket. Then she took out a handkerchief, and began to cry.

'I cannot tell you what to do,' Elinor said. 'You must decide for yourself.'

Lucy took a small picture out of her pocket and showed it to Elinor.

'I suppose that I must,' Lucy said, as tears fell from her eyes. 'But dear Edward is so unhappy. You must have seen that he was sad when he visited you.'

'Yes, we all did,' Elinor replied. She was beginning to believe Lucy now. She also remembered that Edward had come to Barton from Plymouth.

Lucy now took a letter from her pocket.

'This is a letter from Edward,' she said, showing it to Elinor. Lucy's name and an address in Exeter were on it. 'He wrote it to me just before Anne and I came here. Our letters to each other help both of us. Edward does not have a picture of me, but I gave him a lock of my hair. He wears it in a ring. Did you see it?'

'Yes, I did,' Elinor said. She spoke quietly and tried to hide her feelings, but she was very, very unhappy.

The two girls were now outside the Dashwoods' cottage. Lucy said goodbye to Elinor and returned to Barton Park.

Elinor went to her room to think. Everything that Lucy had told her must be true. Edward was engaged to Lucy Steele! But did he love Lucy? Elinor did not believe this. She was sure that Edward loved *her*. He had looked at her with love when he visited Barton.

'Edward's engagement to Lucy is a mistake,' Elinor thought. 'He became engaged four years ago. He was young then – only nineteen. I am sure that he does not love Lucy now. This news has made me unhappy, but Edward must be unhappier. Lucy Steele is uneducated, untruthful and sly and she thinks of no one but herself. She will never make Edward happy.'

As usual, Elinor told no one about her feelings. She could remain strong, but only if she kept her thoughts to herself. Elinor decided to ask Lucy Steele some more questions as soon as she could. Her chance came one evening at Barton Park. Marianne was playing the piano and thinking of

Willoughby. The Middletons and Miss Steele were playing cards. Lucy was sitting at a table alone. She was making a gift for little Annamaria. Elinor walked across the room and sat down beside Lucy.

'When we last met, you told me your secret,' Elinor said. 'I would like to ask you a few questions about it.'

'Of course, my dear Miss Dashwood,' Lucy replied. 'Friends tell each other everything. But I thought that my news had made you unhappy.'

Lucy looked sharply at Elinor. Then she said, 'I am so pleased to share my secret with a true friend. I feel so much happier now.'

'I am sure that you are pleased to share your secret,' Elinor said. 'You and Edward have many problems, I know that. Edward has no profession and very little money of his own. He is very dependent on his mother.'

'That is true,' Lucy replied sadly. 'Edward has only £2000 of his own. It would be very foolish for us to get married without money from his mother. I would not mind being poor if I were with Edward, of course. But I do not want him to lose his mother's money because of me. We must wait. There is no other way.

'Edward has loved me for four years,' Lucy went on. 'He will never stop loving me, I am sure. I would know at once if he did.'

'So what are you going to do?' Elinor asked. 'Are you waiting for Mrs Ferrars to die? How long will you and Edward wait?'

'Mrs Ferrars is a very proud woman,' Lucy said, sighing. 'If we make her angry, she may leave all her money to Robert, Edward's younger brother. That must never happen. It would hurt Edward too much.'

'It would hurt you too,' Elinor said quietly.

Lucy looked at Elinor sharply, but she did not answer her.

Then Elinor asked another question.

'Do you know Mr Robert Ferrars?'

'No, I have never seen him,' Lucy replied. 'I have heard that Robert is very unlike Edward. Robert is foolish and proud.'

Miss Steele had come to their table. She heard these words and laughed.

'Foolish and proud?' she repeated loudly. 'You must be talking about young men!'

'Miss Dashwood's young man is very quiet and he has good manners,' Mrs Jennings called out. 'But who does Miss Lucy love? Is that a secret?'

'Lucy's young man is as quiet and well-mannered as Miss Dashwood's young man,' Anne Steele said quickly.

Elinor's face became red and Lucy frowned angrily at her sister. After a few seconds, Lucy spoke very quietly to Elinor.

'As you may know, Edward wants to be a clergyman,' Lucy said. 'Your brother John could help Edward. John Dashwood could help Edward to become the clergyman in the church at Norland.'

'You should ask his wife, Fanny Dashwood, to help Edward,' Elinor said.

Lucy sighed again. 'Oh, no,' she said. 'She will not help us. Perhaps I should end our engagement. You must help me to make this decision, Miss Dashwood. You must help me with my problem. I will do whatever you say.'

Elinor knew that Lucy was playing a game with her, so she did not reply. Lucy soon spoke again.

'Will you be in London this winter, Miss Dashwood?' Lucy asked.

'No, I will not,' Elinor replied.

'I am sorry to hear that,' Lucy said happily. 'I am going with Anne at the end of January. I am going because Edward will be in London during February.'

Elinor decided not to say anything more about Edward and his engagement to Lucy. But Lucy spoke about Edward whenever she could and this made Elinor feel very unhappy.

The Steeles stayed on at Barton Park for nearly two months. They did not leave until after Christmas.

7

An Invitation From Mrs Jennings

Mrs Jennings loved to meet people and talk to them. The old lady spent many months of each year visiting her friends and relations in their houses in the country. But she always spent the winter months at her home in London. She had a house in Berkeley Street, a fashionable part of London.

Before Charlotte was married, she had lived with her mother. Now Mrs Jennings was alone and she wanted some other young people to talk to. At the end of December, she decided to invite Elinor and Marianne Dashwood to her house in London. She invited them to be her guests there. The Middletons and the Palmers would also be in London at this time.

At first, Elinor refused Mrs Jennings' invitation. She thanked the old lady and said that she would not go. 'I am afraid that I cannot leave my mother and Barton Cottage for such a long time,' she said.

'Your mother will not be lonely!' Mrs Jennings said. 'She has Margaret to look after her. You and Marianne will enjoy London. The Miss Steeles will be coming to London with Sir John and Lady Middleton in the middle of January. My daughters, Lady Middleton and Mrs Palmer, have many friends there and we can visit them all. There are plenty of fine young men in London, you know! At least one of you will be married before the spring, I am sure!'

Marianne did not like these remarks. She thought that Mrs Jennings was a foolish and vulgar old woman. But Marianne also knew that Willoughby would be staying in London that winter. Marianne wanted to see him again. She wanted to find out his true feelings for her. She wanted to accept Mrs Jennings' invitation.

Elinor was afraid of seeing Edward Ferrars and Lucy Steele together in London. That was the true reason why Elinor did not want to go there. But she understood Marianne's feelings. Elinor always thought of other peoples' feelings before her own.

'I know that Mrs Jennings upsets you when she makes remarks about love and young men,' Mrs Dashwood told her daughters. 'She is vulgar, but she has a kind heart. Remember, you will be with Lady Middleton too. Go to London and enjoy yourselves, my dears!'

Then Elinor remembered that Edward would not be in London until February. She began to feel a little happier about the visit. The sisters accepted Mrs Jennings' invitation.

The journey to London took three days. Mrs Jennings looked after her young friends very well during that time.

Mrs Jennings' fine house in Berkeley Street was large and well furnished. Elinor and Marianne were both delighted when they saw the comfortable room that they were going to share. The sisters immediately sat down to write letters.

'I am writing to mama, Marianne,' Elinor said to her sister. 'Why do you not wait a day or two before sending her your letter? You will have more to tell her then.'

'I am not writing to mama,' Marianne said quickly.

Marianne did not say anything more, but Elinor saw the letter W at the beginning of the address. As soon as she had finished writing, Marianne called for a servant. She asked the servant to deliver her letter immediately. She said nothing more to Elinor about the letter, but she was too excited to eat anything at dinner.

Later in the afternoon, when the sisters were drinking tea, there was a loud knock on the front door of the house.

Marianne jumped up from her chair. Her dark eyes were shining with happiness.

'Oh, Elinor, it is Willoughby!' she cried. 'I know that it is!'

The sitting-room door opened. Marianne ran towards it and almost fell into the arms of the man who entered. But the visitor was not Willoughby, it was Colonel Brandon. As soon as Marianne saw who it was, her eyes filled with tears and she ran from the room.

'Is your sister ill?' Colonel Brandon asked.

When Elinor replied that Marianne had a headache, Colonel Brandon looked worried.

The two friends began talking, but their conversation was short and uninteresting. They were both thinking of other things. Elinor wanted to ask the Colonel about Willoughby, and Colonel Brandon could think of no one but Marianne.

Next morning, Charlotte Palmer called to see her mother and her young visitors. Very soon, they all went to Bond Street to visit all the fashionable shops there.

As they walked along the street, Marianne looked for Willoughby. She did not see him and she was disappointed. When they returned to Berkeley Street, Marianne asked a servant if Willoughby had called. But he had not called at the house and there were no letters for Marianne either.

'Why has he not replied to my letter?' said Marianne quietly.

Elinor did not understand what had happened to Willoughby. If Willoughby and Marianne *were* engaged, he should have called on Marianne at Mrs Jennings' house, or he should have written to her.

At breakfast the next morning, Mrs Jennings said, 'The weather is so fine that all the gentlemen must still be in the country. They will be enjoying themselves. They will be hunting. They will not come to London until it gets colder.'

These words made the sisters feel happier.

Marianne was very happy to agree with this idea. 'Of course! Willoughby has not arrived in London yet!' she said to Elinor. 'But the weather is getting colder. Soon, the ground will be hard and frozen with ice. Then the gentlemen will not be able to hunt with their dogs and horses. They will come to London and I will see Willoughby again!'

Marianne was right. A few days later, more gentlemen came to London and Willoughby arrived with them. He called at the house in Berkeley Street when Mrs Jennings and the Dashwoods were out. His visiting card was on the table in the hall when they returned. Marianne picked up the card before Mrs Jennings saw it.

'Look, Elinor! Willoughby called when we were out!' Marianne cried. 'I shall stay here tomorrow. I do not want to miss him again.'

So the next day, Marianne stayed in the house. But Willoughby did not call again and no letter came from him. Elinor saw that her sister was very upset.

'Are you are expecting Willoughby to write to you?' Elinor asked.

'Yes ... no ... perhaps,' Marianne replied. She did not look at her sister.

'You are not telling me everything, Marianne,' Elinor said quietly.

'How can you say that to me?' Marianne cried. 'You tell me nothing about yourself, nothing at all!'

'I have nothing to tell you,' Elinor replied.

'Then neither have I!' Marianne said, with tears in her eyes.

The Middletons had now arrived in London. Sir John at once invited a few young friends, including the Miss Dashwoods, to a dance at his house in Conduit Street.

As soon as they arrived at the Middletons' house, Marianne looked around the drawing-room. But Willoughby was not among the guests and she was not interested in any of the other people there. As they were returning to Berkeley Street, Marianne said that she was very tired.

'And we all know *why* you are tired, Miss Marianne!' Mrs Jennings said, laughing loudly. 'You would not be tired if Willoughby had been there to dance with you! Why was Willoughby not there? He was invited. Sir John told me that himself.'

Marianne said nothing, but she looked very unhappy.

Next morning, after breakfast, Marianne wrote another letter to Willoughby. Elinor was now worried about her sister. Marianne was disappointed and unhappy. Elinor decided to write to her mother and tell her what was happening. Was Marianne engaged to Willoughby or not?

When Colonel Brandon called at midday, he talked to Elinor about Marianne and Willoughby.

'Everyone believes that Willoughby and your sister are engaged,' Colonel Brandon told Elinor sadly.

'But that cannot be true!' Elinor cried. 'I am Marianne's sister and she has told me nothing. She has told no one in our family that she and Willoughby are to be married.'

'Mrs Jennings, Mrs Palmer and the Middletons are all talking about it,' the Colonel replied. 'They believe that Willoughby has asked Marianne to marry him. And as I came in just now, your sister was giving a servant a letter. The letter was addressed to Willoughby.'

'Miss Dashwood,' the Colonel went on quickly, 'I must tell you that I have the strongest feelings for your sister. But if she loves Willoughby, I will say nothing to her. If they have made an arrangement – if they are engaged – I will say no more. Please tell me the truth.'

Elinor did not know what to say to her friend.

'Colonel Brandon, I am sure that my sister loves Willoughby,' she said at last. 'They write to each other. They must be engaged. So Willoughby must love Marianne too.'

When he heard these words, Colonel Brandon stood up.

'Thank you, Miss Dashwood,' he said. 'I hope that your sister will be very happy. Willoughby is a very lucky man. I hope that he understands this. Please do not say anything about my visit and our conversation to anyone.'

And, without another word, the Colonel bowed and left the house.

Three or four days passed. Willoughby did not call and he did not write. Marianne became more and more unhappy.

Then the Dashwood sisters were invited to a very big party at a friend of Lady Middleton's. Lady Middleton took Marianne and Elinor with her in her carriage.

The large house was in a fashionable part of London. It was full of people and the crowded rooms were very hot. The Miss Dashwoods sat down to watch the guests talking, playing cards and dancing.

Suddenly, Elinor saw Willoughby standing in the next room. He was smiling and talking happily to a pretty young woman who was dressed in very fashionable clothes. Willoughby turned and saw Elinor and Marianne. He bowed towards them, but went on talking to the pretty young woman.

At that moment, Marianne saw Willoughby and she stood up. She smiled and her eyes shone with happiness. She began to walk across the room towards Willoughby, but Elinor held her arm.

'Oh, Elinor!' Marianne cried. 'He is here! Oh, why does he not come to me? I must speak to him!'

'Please, Marianne, people are looking at you,' Elinor said. 'Perhaps Willoughby has not seen you yet.'

Then, at last, Willoughby looked again at the sisters and bowed once more. Elinor and Marianne were now only a few feet away from the young man.

'Miss Dashwood,' he said to Elinor, 'how long have you been in London? Is your mother well?'

Marianne ran towards Willoughby, holding her hand out to him. But the young man turned away from her and spoke again to the pretty young woman beside him. Marianne's eyes filled with tears.

'Willoughby, Willoughby! What is the matter?' she cried. 'Did you not receive my letters? Why will you not shake hands with me?'

Other people nearby had now stopped talking. They were watching the four young people and they were listening to their conversation.

Willoughby touched Marianne's hand for a moment.

'I called at Berkeley Street, but you were out,' he said very quietly.

'Did you not receive my letters?' Marianne cried again. 'For God's sake[49], Willoughby! What is the matter?'

'Yes, I received them. Thank you for telling me that you were in London,' Willoughby said quickly. He bowed and moved away to speak to the fashionably-dressed young lady again.

'Elinor, bring him back. I must speak to him,' Marianne said. Her face was now very pale and her body was shaking.

Elinor helped her sister to sit down.

'Nothing can be done now,' Elinor said. 'Wait until

'For God's sake, Willoughby! What is the matter?'

tomorrow, my dear sister.'

A few minutes later, Willoughby left the room and he did not return. Elinor went to Lady Middleton and said that her sister was unwell. She asked if they could return to Berkeley Street.

Marianne said nothing during the journey back to Mrs Jennings' house. Elinor helped her sister to their room and Marianne was soon in bed.

8

Letters

The morning after the dance, Marianne got up very early, sat at a desk by the window, and began writing a letter to Willoughby. It was now the middle of the month of January and the mornings were cold and dark.

As Marianne wrote, she wept loudly and her body shook with the cold. The sound of her crying woke her sister.

'Marianne, may I ask you ... ?' Elinor began.

'No, Elinor,' Marianne replied. 'Do not ask me anything yet. You will soon know everything.'

Elinor understood that Marianne was writing her last letter to Willoughby. There was nothing more that Elinor could say. Marianne soon finished writing the letter and she gave it to a servant. Now she could only wait and hope for a reply.

Willoughby's letter arrived during breakfast. Marianne took it from the servant and ran quickly from the room. She wanted to read it alone.

Mrs Jennings laughed happily. 'I have never seen a girl who is so much in love!' the foolish old lady said. 'I hope that Willoughby does not want a long engagement. When are they going to be married, Miss Dashwood?'

'I am not sure that Marianne and Willoughby *are* engaged,' Elinor replied quickly. 'They have not talked about marriage.'

Mrs Jennings laughed again and shook her head.

'How can you say that, Miss Dashwood?' she said. 'Those two young people were in love from the first moment that they met! Everyone knows that Miss Marianne came to London to buy her wedding-clothes!'

This is what Mrs Jennings believed. She would not listen to any other ideas. Elinor did not say anything more but sat politely at the table. At last Mrs Jennings finished eating her breakfast, and Elinor ran upstairs to her sister.

Marianne was lying on her bed in their room, weeping loudly. There was a letter in her hand and other letters lay on the bed beside her. When Marianne saw Elinor, she put all the letters into her sister's hands and then turned away.

Elinor opened Willoughby's letter and read it quickly.

Bond Street
January

My Dear Madam,

I have just received your letter. You say that I have upset you by my behaviour and that I have treated you badly[50]*. I am sorry that you think this and I apologise. I never wanted to upset you or your family, and I remember with pleasure our friendship at Barton.*

I am afraid that you misunderstood that friendship. My feelings were not as strong as yours. I was never in love with you. I have loved another lady for some time and I shall soon be engaged to her. I am therefore doing what you asked. I am returning all your letters. I am also returning the lock of hair that you kindly gave me.

Yours most sincerely,
John Willoughby

It was a very cold, unkind letter and every word had hurt poor Marianne very much. Elinor read Willoughby's cruel words again and again. At first she was too angry to speak. She did not know what to say to her sister. Her eyes filled with tears.

'Poor Elinor, how unhappy I have made you!' Marianne said at last. 'My unhappiness has made you unhappy too.'

As she said this, Marianne began to cry more loudly than before.

'Dear Marianne, please stop crying,' Elinor told her sister kindly. 'You will make yourself ill and upset all your friends and family.'

'I am not like you, Elinor. I cannot hide my feelings!' Marianne replied. 'If you do not want to see my tears, please leave me alone. You cannot understand how I am feeling.

'Sensible Elinor,' Marianne went on. 'You have your Edward and you can look forward to a life of happiness with him. I have lost my Willoughby for ever.'

'I am not sure that Edward loves me,' Elinor said. 'I have heard stories. I have been told ... '

'No, no!' Marianne cried. 'Edward loves you, only you. You cannot understand unhappiness like mine. I shall never be happy again – never!'

'Please do not say that,' Elinor said quickly. 'You have many good friends and a family that loves you. If your engagement had gone on any longer, things would have been much worse.'

'Engagement?' said Marianne. 'There was no engagement.'

'But surely Willoughby told you that he loved you?'

'Yes ... well ... No, not exactly,' Marianne said. 'He never said the words, "I love you." But everything that he said and did made me believe that he loved me.'

'But you wrote to him, Marianne. If you were not engaged, that was very wrong.'

'I shall never be happy again – never!'

'No, it was not wrong. You must not say that, Elinor. But I cannot talk to you about that now.'

Elinor did not reply. She picked up the three letters that Marianne had written and began to read them.

The first had been written on the day that they had arrived in London. Marianne had written Mrs Jennings' address in Berkeley Street at the top of the letter.

I am sure that you will be surprised when you read this, Willoughby. I am in London! I am staying with Mrs Jennings. I look forward to seeing you tomorrow. M.D.

The second letter had been written after the Middletons' dance.

You called here the day before yesterday. I was out. I am so sorry that I did not see you. I wrote to you a week ago and you still have not answered my letter. I expected to see you at Lady Middleton's dance last night. Why were you not at her house in Conduit Street? You must want to see me, as much as I want to see you. Come soon. M.D.

In her third letter to Willoughby, Marianne had written:

I cannot understand the way that you behaved last night. You must explain your cruel treatment of me.

I spoke to you as a loving friend and you turned away from me. Why? Why have your feelings for me changed? Or have I misunderstood your behaviour from the day that we met?

If that is the truth – though I cannot believe it – you must return my letters. And please return the lock of my hair that you asked for at a happier time. M.D.

Marianne waited until her sister had read the letters and then she spoke.

'I loved Willoughby and Willoughby felt the same about me,' she said. 'I know that he loved me. I *felt* that I was engaged to him. But someone has changed him. Someone has made him cruel. I have an enemy, but it is not Willoughby.'

'Then show the enemy your pride, my dear sister!' Elinor said. 'Be strong. Do not let your enemy see your unhappiness.'

'No, no. I am too unhappy to have any pride,' Marianne replied. 'I cannot look happy when I am not. Oh, Elinor, I am so miserable. Please, let us go home to mama. Let us go home to Barton tomorrow!'

'No, Marianne, we cannot do that.'

'Then we must go home in a day or two. Mrs Jennings and Lady Middleton will ask me lots of questions that I will not want to answer. They will feel sorry for me and that will make me more unhappy.'

Before Elinor could reply, Mrs Jennings herself came into the room.

'How are you, my dear Marianne?' she asked. But the unhappy girl could not answer.

'Poor Miss Marianne,' Mrs Jennings said to Elinor. 'I have just come back from a visit to my friend, Mrs Taylor. And while I was there, I heard some news about Willoughby.'

Marianne began to cry again, so Elinor and Mrs Jennings left her alone. As they walked downstairs, Mrs Jennings went on talking.

'Willoughby is going to be married very soon – to Miss Sofia Grey. Miss Grey is not as beautiful as Marianne, but she is pretty and has £50,000 of her own.

'Willoughby has behaved very badly,' Mrs Jennings went on, 'but he needs Miss Grey's money. Young men cannot live without money, you know. But perhaps this news about Willoughby will be good luck for Colonel Brandon!'

9

Colonel Brandon's Story

Colonel Brandon was a visitor at Mrs Jennings' house soon after Willoughby returned Marianne's letters. The first person who Brandon asked about was Marianne. But she did not come downstairs. She was too unhappy to speak to visitors.

'Marianne is not well and she is in bed,' Elinor told him.

'Then I am afraid that the news I heard this morning may be true,' said the Colonel in a worried voice.

'You are talking about Mr Willoughby's engagement to Miss Grey,' Elinor said, very quietly.

'Yes. I believe that they are to be married in a few weeks. How is your sister? What does she feel about the news?' the Colonel asked.

'The news has upset her very much,' Elinor replied. 'She wants to think well of Willoughby, but that is very difficult, of course.'

The Colonel did not answer and he left the house soon afterwards.

A day or two later, Colonel Brandon called again when Mrs Jennings was out. After politely greeting the Colonel, Marianne apologised to him and went upstairs to her room.

The Colonel and Elinor were alone in the drawing-room. Colonel Brandon sat down beside her and, after a while, he began to speak.

'I am pleased that we can speak alone, Miss Dashwood,' he said. 'There is something that I want to tell you. It is about Willoughby. The story is an unhappy one, but I believe that your sister should know it. I think that it will help her.

She will not want to hear the story from me, so I should like to tell it to you, Miss Dashwood.'

'Please continue, Colonel Brandon,' Elinor said. 'I should very much like to hear this story.'

'My story begins some time ago,' the Colonel said. 'It is about a lady. She was an orphan – her parents died when she was a young girl. Her name was Eliza Williams. When Eliza's parents died, my father brought her to live in our house. I was a very young man and I fell in love with Eliza at once. And she loved me. Eliza was beautiful and intelligent. She loved art, poetry, music and literature. She had strong feelings about love and life. I was reminded of Eliza the first time that I saw your sister, Marianne.

'Eliza was not only beautiful, she was also very rich. When she was seventeen, she had to marry my elder brother. My family needed money to make repairs to our house at Delaford. So my father made Eliza marry my brother. I could do nothing. Soon after the marriage, my father died, and I joined the army. I went to India.

'Two years later, I heard that the marriage between Eliza and my brother was over,' Colonel Brandon went on. 'My brother and Eliza were divorced[51]. My brother had been very cruel to Eliza. He had beaten her. She had run away with another man.

'I could not return to England for another three years. But when I came back, I looked everywhere for Eliza. I did not find her for six months. By that time, she had no money and she was very ill – she was dying. I put her in a comfortable place, with servants to look after her. I visited her every day and I was with her when she died.

'Eliza left me her little girl who was then about three years old. She had named her daughter, Eliza, too. I promised to look after little Eliza and I sent her to school when she was old enough. I was happy to do this.'

'After my brother died, I inherited Delaford and little Eliza often visited me there,' said Brandon. 'When Eliza was fourteen – about three years ago – she went to live with a very good woman in the county of Dorset. Last February, Eliza went to the town of Bath, with one of her friends. Then she disappeared for eight months. Later, I learnt that she had left Bath with a young man.'

The Colonel stopped speaking and looked sadly at Elinor.

'Good heavens!' Elinor cried. She had guessed the truth. 'Do you mean that the young man was Willoughby?'

'Yes. That young man was John Willoughby,' Brandon said quietly. 'I did not hear from Eliza until October. I was staying with the Middletons at Barton Park. Her letter was sent on to me there from Delaford. It gave me terrible news. I had to leave Barton at once. I could not take you all on the visit to Whitwell – my brother-in-law's house.

'When I reached Eliza in London,' Brandon continued, 'she was in terrible trouble. She was expecting a child – Willoughby's child. He had seduced[52] her, spent her money, and left her. She never saw him again.'

'This is terrible news!' Elinor cried.

'Now you understand Willoughby's true character,' Colonel Brandon said. 'You can understand my feelings when I saw him with your sister at Barton. And this man has now deceived[53] Marianne.'

'Have you seen Mr Willoughby since you left him at Barton?' Elinor asked.

'Yes. We met once,' the Colonel said. 'Willoughby had to be punished and so we fought together. We fought a duel[54]. I am a soldier and I can shoot very well. Neither of us was wounded during the duel, and our meeting is still a secret.'

'And what happened to Eliza?' Elinor asked.

'She gave birth to her child and they are now both living in the country,' Colonel Brandon replied.

'But I have kept you from your poor sister for too long,' he went on. 'I ask you to tell her this sad story. She should know the truth. I am sure that you agree.'

Elinor told Marianne the Colonel's story the next day. Marianne said very little when she heard about Eliza and Willoughby, and she did not cry. But Eliza's story had made Marianne very unhappy. She believed every word of it.

Soon after the Colonel's visit, Marianne felt stronger and she left her room. Sometimes, she smiled and spoke a few words to Brandon when he visited.

Elinor wrote to their mother and told her the whole story of Willoughby and young Eliza Williams. Mrs Dashwood was upset. But she told her daughters that they should stay in London for a few more weeks. Barton Cottage would only remind Marianne of happier times with Willoughby.

Mrs Dashwood had also heard that Mr and Mrs John Dashwood would soon be in London. They had rented a house in Harley Street for a few months. Mrs Dashwood wanted Elinor and Marianne to see their brother again. She wanted her daughters to be friends with him and Fanny.

The Dashwood sisters were now thinking of each other's feelings. Marianne was staying in London to help her sister. Elinor was staying to help Marianne. And Elinor was very careful not to speak about Willoughby when Marianne was in the room. Even Mrs Jennings and Charlotte Palmer said nothing about Willoughby when they were with Marianne.

Early in February, Willoughby and Miss Grey were married. They left London at once and travelled to Willoughby's home in Somerset. When Marianne heard this news, she stayed in her room all day and wept many tears. But after a few days, she was able to leave the house and meet people again.

Sometimes, Marianne smiled and spoke a few words to Brandon when he visited.

10

The Ferrars Family

Anne and Lucy Steele were now staying in London with the Middletons. Everyone except Elinor was pleased to see them. The Steeles soon called on Mrs Jennings at her house in Berkeley Street. When Lucy saw Elinor there, she went up to her at once.

'I am so pleased that you are still in London, Miss Dashwood,' Lucy said with a sly smile. 'You told me that you would only stay a month, but I knew that you would stay longer. And now that your brother is coming to London you will not want to leave at all! Will you be staying with Mr and Mrs Dashwood when they arrive?'

'No, I do not think so,' Elinor replied.

'Oh, I am sure that you will!' Lucy cried. 'But you have been away from home such a long time! What does your mother think about that?'

Mrs Jennings heard Lucy's remark and spoke immediately. 'Oh! The Miss Dashwoods' visit has only just begun!' the old lady said kindly. 'I want them to stay as my guests for as long as possible.'

'I hear that Miss Marianne Dashwood has been ill,' Lucy went on. 'What is the matter with her? Where is she?'

'My sister has a headache today and she is resting in our room,' Elinor replied quietly.

'Then we must go and see her!' Anne Steele cried and she began to walk quickly towards the door.

'Please let her rest,' Elinor said.

Lucy frowned at her sister when she saw that Elinor was angry. Anne Steele said nothing more.

The following morning, Elinor persuaded Marianne to go with her to Bond Street. Elinor took some of her mother's jewellery that needed to be repaired. The small jeweller's shop was very crowded and busy, so the Miss Dashwoods sat down to wait.

Elinor noticed a handsome young man in the shop. He was talking to the jeweller. The young gentleman was about twenty-three years old and he was dressed in fine, fashionable clothes. Elinor had not seen the gentleman before, but his face reminded her of someone else.

The young man spent a long time in the shop and bought several things. He did not speak to Elinor and Marianne, but he looked at them before he left.

Elinor's business in the shop was over quickly. Just as the sisters were leaving, their brother, Mr John Dashwood, came in. He bowed politely and seemed pleased to see them.

'Fanny and I have been in town for two days, but we have had no time to call on you,' John told Elinor and Marianne. 'We spent most of yesterday with Fanny's mother, Mrs Ferrars. But I shall certainly call on Mrs Jennings tomorrow. We should like to meet the Middletons too. I believe that they have been good friends to you in Devon.'

'Yes, they have,' Elinor replied. 'They have been very kind to us. And we often visit them here in London.'

'I am very pleased to hear it,' John Dashwood replied with a smile. 'The Middletons are very rich and they are members of our family too. Edward has told Fanny and me how kind the Middletons are.'

John Dashwood came to Berkeley Street the next day to call on Mrs Jennings. Colonel Brandon was also visiting that morning.

After staying for half an hour, John Dashwood asked Elinor to introduce him to the Middletons. On the way to the Middletons' house, John asked his sister questions about the Colonel.

'Who is Colonel Brandon?' he asked. 'I could see that he is a gentleman. Is he rich?'

'He has a large house in Dorset,' Elinor replied, smiling.

'I am very pleased to hear it,' her brother said. 'Elinor, I congratulate you. You have done well.'

'What do you mean, John?' Elinor asked in surprise.

'Well, Colonel Brandon is interested in you. He likes you, I am sure of it,' John replied. '*Is* Brandon rich?'

'He has £2000 a year, I believe,' Elinor said.

'Well, I wish that his fortune were bigger, sister. But you will have enough money and a good house to live in too.'

'You are wrong, brother,' Elinor said quickly. 'Colonel Brandon has no thought of marrying me.'

John Dashwood smiled. 'I know that you have little money, Elinor,' he said. 'But do not be worried by that. Try to catch the Colonel! No one else wants to marry you, we all know that. A marriage between you and Brandon will please everyone. I know that Mrs Ferrars will be delighted to hear about it! If you *and* Edward are both married to suitable people, it will please her and everyone in your family.'

'Is Mr Edward Ferrars going to be married?' Elinor asked quickly.

'His mother certainly hopes so. She has found him a most suitable lady. Her name is Miss Morton. She is the daughter of a rich lord. She has £30,000 a year!

'If Edward marries Miss Morton, Mrs Ferrars will give him £1000 a year,' John went on. 'Mrs Ferrars is a very generous woman. She gave Fanny two hundred pounds yesterday, to help with our expenses here in London.'

'But you have plenty of money, brother,' Elinor replied.

'Perhaps,' John said. 'But we have many expenses, both here and in the country. We have spent a lot of money to make Norland Park more comfortable. And there is a lot more work to be done.'

Elinor could not think of a polite reply and her brother went on talking, this time about Marianne.

'What is the matter with Marianne?' John Dashwood asked. 'She used to be a very pretty girl. Fanny used to say that Marianne would make a better marriage than you. But your sister has changed so much. She looks quite ill. No one suitable will be interested in her now!'

Elinor and her brother had now reached the Middletons' house in Conduit Street. Sir John and Lady Middleton were both at home and John Dashwood was delighted to meet them. He believed that his sisters had done well to make friends with the Middletons and Mrs Jennings. They were all important members of society, and they were very rich. And now they were his friends too.

Fanny – Mrs John Dashwood – soon called on the Middletons and Mrs Jennings. Fanny and Lady Middleton were very much alike. There were interested in the same things – money, their position in society, and their children. They soon became good friends.

Not long after this, Elinor heard that Edward Ferrars had come to London with John and Fanny. He called twice at Mrs Jennings' house. But each time that he visited, Elinor was out. She was pleased that Edward had called, but she was happy not to have seen him.

Mr and Mrs John Dashwood decided to give a dinner party at which the Middletons would be the most important guests. Elinor and Marianne were invited, together with Mrs Jennings and Colonel Brandon. Lucy Steele and her sister were staying with the Middletons, so, of course, they would be at the dinner party too.

Fanny's mother, Mrs Ferrars, was going to be another of the guests. Elinor thought that Edward would be coming with his mother. But she was wrong. As soon as Lucy saw Elinor, she was happy to tell her the reason why.

'My dear Edward will not be at the Dashwoods' dinner on Tuesday,' Lucy said. 'He is not going because he would not be able to hide his feelings for me. Oh! My dear Miss Dashwood! I shall be meeting Edward's mother for the first time! Mrs Ferrars – the lady who will soon be my mother-in-law! How frightened I am!' As she said this, Lucy looked at Elinor slyly.

Elinor very much wanted to tell Lucy about Mrs Ferrar's plans for Edward and Miss Morton, but she did not. Instead, she said, 'I feel very sorry for you, Lucy.'

Mrs Ferrars was a small, thin woman with pale skin. Her plain face had a proud, angry look and she did not speak to Elinor and Marianne at all. But the old lady smiled at the Steele sisters. Mrs Ferrars had no idea that Lucy was hoping to marry her eldest son.

The Dashwoods gave their guests a fine dinner. There were many servants to serve the very best food and wine. The meal continued for many hours.

Later in the evening, when all the guests were in the drawing-room, John Dashwood showed Colonel Brandon a very pretty pair of screens[55].

'The pictures on the screens were painted by my sister, Elinor, and given to Fanny,' John Dashwood said. 'They are very well painted, do you not think?'

The Colonel agreed and the pieces of furniture were shown to the other guests. Mrs Ferrars asked to see them. But when she was told that the screens were Elinor's work, she would not look at them.

Fanny was embarrassed by her mother's bad manners.

'Do look at the screens, mama. They are very pretty,' Fanny said. 'Elinor paints almost as well as Miss Morton.

And Miss Morton paints very well indeed, as you know.'

'Miss Morton does everything well. She has the best teachers,' Mrs Ferrars said, frowning at Elinor as she spoke.

Marianne was very upset by Mrs Ferrars' unkind words. 'These screens were painted by my dear sister, Elinor,' she said. 'Who cares about Miss Morton's work – or Miss Morton?'

'We all care about Miss Morton,' Mrs Ferrars said coldly and angrily. 'She is Lord Morton's daughter.'

Marianne's eyes filled with tears and she walked across to her sister. 'Elinor dear,' she said. 'Do not let them make you unhappy. We both know how cruel people can be.'

Then Lady Middleton began to talk of other things and the rest of the evening passed quietly.

Lucy Steele called at Mrs Jennings' house early the following morning. She immediately sat beside Elinor.

'My dear friend, I have come to talk to you about my happiness,' Lucy said. 'Mrs Ferrars talked to me for some time yesterday evening. I think that she likes me. It is so important to my dear Edward and myself.'

'Mrs Ferrars was certainly polite to you,' Elinor replied.

'Polite!' Lucy repeated. 'Mrs Ferrars was more than polite to me. She was very kind. And your sister, Mrs Dashwood, was very kind too.'

'Neither Mrs Ferrars, nor Mrs Dashwood, have been told about your engagement, have they?' Elinor said.

'No,' Lucy said, 'but it will not change their feelings towards me. Mrs Ferrars is a very kind woman and so is Mrs Dashwood.'

Elinor could not agree with this, so she did not reply.

'Are you ill, Miss Dashwood?' Lucy asked with a smile. 'Is that why you are not answering me? I do hope that you are not ill. I need your friendship at this time. Next to Edward's love for me, your friendship is the greatest help to me.'

At that moment, the drawing-door door opened and a servant said, 'Mr Ferrars.' Two seconds later, Edward Ferrars walked into the room.

All three young people were embarrassed. Elinor spoke first. She asked Edward to sit down and started to talk to him about their time in London. But Edward did not join in the conversation. He sat in silence.

'I am sure that Marianne would like to see you, Edward,' Elinor said at last. 'Let me go and find her.'

Elinor walked upstairs very slowly. She wanted Edward and Lucy to have time to talk to each other.

When Marianne heard that Edward had arrived, she was delighted. She ran downstairs into the drawing-room.

'Dear Edward, how happy I am to see you!' she cried, smiling. She held out her hand to the young man. She smiled again, first at Edward and then at her sister.

'You look pale and tired, Miss Marianne,' Edward said at last. 'Perhaps you are not happy in London.'

'Oh, do not worry about me!' Marianne cried. 'Elinor is well. That is the important thing. We are both delighted to see you again, Edward. My sister and I shall be returning to Barton very soon. I hope that you will be able to go with us. That would be a great help.'

Lucy frowned angrily at these words, but she did not know what to say.

'Why were you not at the Middletons' yesterday, Edward?' Marianne asked the young man.

'I had another engagement,' Edward said quietly. 'I had been invited to another place. It was an important invitation.'

Lucy smiled. 'Some young men keep engagements and others do not!' she said, laughing. 'You know that, Marianne!'

Elinor was very angry, but Marianne smiled at Lucy's cruel words.

All three young people were embarrassed.

'I know that Edward will never do or say anything that is unkind,' Marianne said. 'He will always behave correctly.'

A few minutes later, Edward stood up and walked towards the door.

'My dear Edward,' Marianne said to him very quietly, 'do not go. Lucy will soon be leaving.'

But Edward apologised and said that he could not stay longer. After a few minutes, Lucy went too.

Marianne knew nothing about Edward and Lucy's secret engagement. Elinor had promised Lucy that she would say nothing about it. She had to keep Lucy's secret.

11

The Secret is Out

A few days later, Charlotte Palmer, Mrs Jennings' younger daughter, gave birth to her first child – a son. Mrs Jennings was delighted, and she now spent many hours each day with her daughter and new grandchild.

When Sir John Middleton heard the news, he hurried to Mrs Jennings' house in Berkeley Street. He had an invitation for the Miss Dashwoods.

'My dear Miss Dashwood,' he said to Elinor, 'you and your sister must not stay here by yourselves. While Mrs Jennings is with Charlotte, you must spend every day with us in Conduit Street. Anne and Lucy will be pleased to see you and so will Lady Middleton.'

Elinor was too polite to refuse the invitation. But no one was happy with Sir John's idea, except Mrs Jennings and Sir John himself.

Mrs Jennings thought that the Dashwood sisters and the

Steele sisters were the best of friends. Sir John Middleton did not understand that his wife did not like Elinor and Marianne Dashwood. Lady Middleton thought that the Dashwoods were too clever, and that they read too many books. She liked Anne and Lucy Steele because the sisters flattered her and her badly-behaved children.

Anne and Lucy Steele did not like the Miss Dashwoods because both Elinor and Marianne were pretty and honest. The Dashwoods thought that the Miss Steeles were silly and vulgar.

As usual, Elinor was able to hide her feelings and she was always polite to the Steeles. But Marianne could not hide her feelings easily. She always said what she thought. And now the four girls had to meet every day.

One evening, at a party at the Middletons' house in Conduit Street, all four young women met Mr Robert Ferrars. Elinor recognised him immediately. He was the handsome young man whom she had seen in the jeweller's shop in Bond Street.

Robert Ferrars was unlike his elder brother, Edward. Robert was good-looking and confident. He was dressed in expensive, fashionable clothes and he never stopped talking.

He bowed to Elinor, smiled, and began talking to her.

'You know my elder brother, Edward, I believe,' he said with a laugh. 'He visited you and your family in your little cottage in Devon. If I had enough money, I would buy a little cottage. But I should want to live much closer to London. My brother Edward likes the country, of course. He does not like meeting people, and I do. Edward and I are very different, Miss Dashwood.'

Elinor agreed.

'Yes, Edward is shy,' Robert Ferrars continued. 'It is our mother's fault that he is so uncomfortable when he meets strangers. She made a mistake when he was a boy. I have told

Robert Ferrars was unlike his elder brother, Edward.

her this many times. She sent Edward to a private tutor in Plymouth, but I went to Westminster School in London.

'At Westminster there were many students and I had many friends,' Robert went on. 'I can talk to anyone, as you see. But poor Edward will sometimes sit silently for a whole evening. My brother is not confident. He cannot talk easily when there are large groups of people. He will never change now.'

Elinor was very pleased to hear that, but she did not tell Robert.

When John Dashwood saw Robert Ferrars talking to Elinor, he had an idea.

'Perhaps we should ask my sisters to stay with us for a time, my dear Fanny,' John said to his wife. 'It would help them to meet the best people while they are in London. What do you think, my dear?'

Fanny did not like the idea at all.

'My dear, I would ask them, of course. But I have decided to invite Anne and Lucy Steele to stay here with us for a few days,' Fanny replied. 'My mother is very fond of them and dear little Harry loves them. We can invite your sisters at any time.'

As always, John Dashwood agreed with his wife and the next day, Fanny sent an invitation to Lucy Steele. Lucy showed Fanny's letter to Elinor as soon as she received it.

'This invitation makes me feel hopeful for the future,' Lucy said. 'Fanny is Edward's sister and now she has invited me to stay in her house in Harley Street. I shall often meet Mrs Ferrars there – and my dear Edward too, of course.'

Anne and Lucy Steele had flattered Lady Middleton and now they flattered Mrs John Dashwood. Fanny Dashwood was delighted with the Miss Steeles and she hoped that they would stay as long as possible.

Two weeks after the birth of her son, Mrs Palmer was well and strong again. So Mrs Jennings no longer spent all her time at the Palmers' house in Hanover Square. Elinor and Marianne were delighted to leave the Middletons' house and return to Mrs Jennings' house in Berkeley Street.

Lucy Steele was very happy in the Dashwoods' house in Harley Street. She was already thinking of Fanny Dashwood as her sister-in-law, as well as her friend. But things did not happen as she had hoped.

One day, Mrs Jennings came to Elinor with a piece of gossip that she had just heard.

'My dear Miss Dashwood!' Mrs Jennings cried. 'You will never believe my news! I could not believe it myself at first.'

'What is it, ma'am?' Elinor asked in surprise.

'You will never believe it!' the old lady said again. 'Mr Edward Ferrars has been secretly engaged to my cousin, Lucy Steele, for more than a year! And no one knew about it except her sister, Anne! This is what happened. This is how the secret came out.

'Yesterday, Fanny Dashwood and Anne Steele were sitting together,' Mrs Jennings went on. 'Fanny began to talk about her brother, Edward, marrying Lord Morton's daughter. As you know, Anne and Lucy were warmly welcomed into Fanny's house. Fanny became especially fond of Lucy. She was pleasant to her and gave her gifts. Perhaps Anne thought that she had to tell Fanny the truth about Edward and Lucy. So the foolish young woman told Fanny Dashwood about Lucy's secret.

' "My dear Fanny," Anne told Fanny, with a laugh. "Your brother Edward cannot marry Miss Morton. He is already engaged to my sister, Lucy. I know how happy you will be to hear their secret, now that we are all friends!"

'When Fanny heard the news, she began crying and

screaming at Anne – everyone in the house could hear her!' Mrs Jennings continued. 'John Dashwood hurried into the room and then Lucy ran in. Fanny saw Lucy and began screaming at her. She called Lucy "wicked and sly" and told her and her sister to leave the house at once. Lucy nearly fainted[56] and Anne wept loudly. But Fanny would not take back her words. Anne and Lucy Steele were out of the house in less than an hour. John Dashwood sent for the doctor, and then he sent for his mother-in-law, Mrs Ferrars.

'I feel sorry for Edward and Lucy,' the kind-hearted Mrs Jennings said. 'Mrs Ferrars thinks far too much about herself and about money. If Edward and Lucy are in love, is it wrong that they should marry?'

As she heard Mrs Jennings tell this story, Elinor felt very sorry for Edward too. But she did not feel sorry for Lucy. Elinor believed that Edward would marry Lucy, although his mother did not want this to happen. Elinor decided that Marianne had to hear the news at once, but she had to hear it from Elinor herself.

At first, when she heard Elinor's story, Marianne thought that Edward was as cruel as Willoughby. But a few seconds later, she changed her mind. Marianne had always liked Edward. She believed that he loved Elinor and she knew that Elinor loved him. Marianne was sure of one thing. She had never liked Lucy Steele. Now she hated her.

'How long have you known about this engagement, Elinor?' Marianne asked. 'Did Edward write and tell you about it?'

'No, he did not,' Elinor replied. 'Lucy told me when we were all at Barton. She told me about it four months ago. She made me promise to keep the engagement a secret. And I did.'

'You have known about this engagement for four months!' Marianne repeated in surprise. 'You are very strong Elinor, and you keep your feelings hidden. But this secret must have made you very unhappy. I know that you love Edward.'

'Yes, I do love him, Marianne, but my love has to be a secret too. I do not want to hurt Edward. He will behave like a gentleman, I am sure. He will marry Lucy. He made a promise to her before he met me. Edward and Lucy may have a happy life together. I do not know. I *do* know that I have been very unhappy for the past four months.'

'Oh, Elinor! I have been selfish!' Marianne cried. 'All these months, you have been helping me and I should have been helping you. I am a bad sister. I have been thinking only about myself and I am sorry.'

The sisters agreed to say nothing about their feelings to anyone. They found that very difficult when their brother came to see them the next morning.

'Sisters, you have heard the terrible news, I am sure,' John began. 'My dear wife is still feeling very ill, but please do not worry. The doctor says that she will be better very soon.

'Mrs Ferrars is very upset and she is very angry with Edward,' John Dashwood went on. 'My mother-in-law wished Edward to marry a rich woman from a good family. She had found a suitable young woman – Miss Morton. Miss Morton is very rich, as you know. As soon as she heard about the secret engagement, Mrs Ferrars sent for Edward at once. When he reached her house in Park Street, she told him to end his engagement to Lucy Steele. But he refused to do this. Mrs Ferrars first offered Edward money, then she said that she would take all his money away. But Edward would not change his mind.'

'Who can believe it!' Marianne said. But her brother did not understand her.

'Your surprise at Edward's behaviour is quite correct,' John Dashwood said.

'*I* think that Edward Ferrars has behaved very well,' Mrs Jennings said. 'My cousin, Lucy Steele, is a good girl who should marry a good husband. Edward has thought of Lucy's feelings and he has behaved like an honest man!'

'An honest man!' John Dashwood repeated. 'No, Edward has not behaved honestly. He has made an unsuitable engagement and he kept this a secret. Now he has refused to obey his mother.

'But Edward will wish that he had not behaved in this way,' John Dashwood went on. 'Mrs Ferrars has sent him away. Her younger son, Robert, is now her heir and he will inherit all her money. Edward will have nothing. I feel sorry for him, but it is his own fault.'

After John Dashwood had left her house, Mrs Jennings had many things to say to her young friends about the news. They were all very sorry for Edward and they thought that Mrs Ferrars had behaved very badly.

A few days later, Mrs Jennings and Elinor were walking together in a London park when they saw a young woman walking towards them.

'Look, there is Miss Steele,' Mrs Jennings said to Elinor. 'Go and talk to her. She is sure to tell you everything about Edward and Lucy.'

Mrs Jennings walked away to speak to a friend and Miss Steele walked up to Elinor.

'I am so pleased to see you, Miss Dashwood!' Anne Steele cried. 'You have heard the news, of course. I am afraid that Lucy was angry with me because I told Mrs John Dashwood about the engagement! People have been saying such bad things about Lucy and Edward. I am sure that you have heard the gossip.'

'I have heard nothing,' Elinor replied.

'Well, I can tell you the truth,' Anne said. 'We are now staying in Bartlett's Buildings. My uncle, Mr Pratt, has an apartment there. We did not hear from Edward for three days and Lucy wept all that time. Then Edward came back to London today and we are all happy!

'After leaving his mother's house in Park Street, Edward went into the country,' Anne Steele said. 'He stayed there all of Thursday and Friday. Then he decided to come back to us. Dear Edward! I heard every word that he said to Lucy.

'At first, Edward said that he was too poor to marry. Then Lucy said that she did not mind being poor, as long as she had love. Are those not beautiful words, Miss Dashwood? Then they moved away from the door and I could not hear any more.'

'What do you mean, Miss Steele?' Elinor said. 'Are you saying that you listened to their private conversation?'

'Well, they would not be talking about love if I was in the room!' Miss Steele said with a laugh. 'Lucy would listen at a door if I was talking about love with a young man, I am sure!'

'I am sure that she would,' Elinor said quietly, but Miss Steele did not hear this.

'Edward has decided to became a clergyman,' Anne Steele continued. 'He is going to be ordained[57] as soon as possible. Then he will look for a church where he can live and work. I know that Edward and Lucy will be happy!'

Elinor could not agree with this, but she said nothing.

'Well, I must go,' Miss Steele said. 'Please give my best wishes to Mrs Jennings and Miss Marianne. Perhaps we shall all meet when Lucy and Edward are married!' And, with another foolish laugh, Miss Anne Steele walked away.

The next morning, Elinor had a letter from Lucy herself.

My Dear Miss Dashwood,

I am writing to you as a friend. I want to tell you about my dear Edward and myself. We have both been very unhappy, but now all is well.

I spent two hours with Edward yesterday afternoon. He is

not afraid of his mother's anger, because he has my love. We will have love, but no money! Before we can marry, Edward must be ordained and find a church to work in.

My dear friend – can you, Mrs Jennings, your brother John, or Mr Palmer, help Edward? If you know a suitable church where he can be a clergyman, we could live happily for ever.

I must end this letter now. Please give my best wishes to dear Mrs Jennings. I hope that she will come and see me soon. I also send my best wishes to Miss Marianne, Sir John and Lady Middleton and their dear, dear children.

I am your very dear and true friend,
Lucy Steele

Elinor showed the letter to Mrs Jennings, because that was what Lucy wished.

'Poor Lucy,' the kind old lady said. 'She has written a very good letter and I shall go and visit her. I hope that someone will be able to help Lucy and Edward soon. I feel sorry for them both.'

12

Colonel Brandon Offers His Help

It was now the beginning of March, and the Miss Dashwoods had been in London for more than two months. Marianne wished for the peace and quiet of Barton, and now Elinor wanted to go home too. Their journey would take several days. Elinor began to think carefully about where they would stay when they stopped each evening.

Then Mrs Jennings had an idea which would make the journey easier for the sisters. At the end of March, Thomas and Charlotte Palmer and their son were going to return to Cleveland – their house in the county of Somerset. Mrs Jennings suggested that Elinor and Marianne could travel with the Palmers and stay at Cleveland for a few days on their way home.

At first, this idea upset Marianne very much.

'Cleveland is in Somerset – I cannot go there,' she said. 'It is the county where Willoughby has his home. Remember, I looked forward to living there with him. No, Elinor, I cannot go there.'

'But Cleveland is not near Coombe Magna – Willoughby's house,' Elinor said. 'The Palmers' house is in another part of Somerset. Our journey will be much easier if we stay with the Palmers and rest at their home, before we continue on to Barton. If we travel with them, we will be at home with mama in about three weeks.'

Marianne wanted to see her mother very much, so she soon agreed with the plan.

Mrs Jennings had become very fond of Elinor and Marianne, and she told Colonel Brandon this the following day.

'Ah, Colonel, I do not know what we shall all do without the Miss Dashwoods,' she said. 'How lonely we shall both be!'

The old lady was now sure that the Colonel wanted to marry Elinor. She watched them as they sat talking together and she smiled.

'The Colonel has come to ask Elinor to marry him,' Mrs Jennings said to herself.

However, Colonel Brandon was talking to Elinor about something very different. He had come to talk to her about Edward Ferrars and his mother.

'Mrs Ferrars has behaved very badly towards Edward and Lucy,' the Colonel said. 'I have met Mr Ferrars and I like him. I know that he is your friend too. I have heard that he is going to be ordained. If that is true, I can help him. I can offer Mr Ferrars a position[58] as the curate in the church at Delaford. The curate's house beside the church is small and Mr Ferrars will not earn more than £200 a year. But if he wants the position, he can have it. Perhaps you would tell him, Miss Dashwood.'

Elinor was delighted and thanked the Colonel for his kindness.

'I am sure that Mr Ferrars will accept your offer,' she said. 'He will not disappoint you. He is a good and honest young man. When he is married, the curate's house will be big enough for him and his wife, I am sure.'

The Colonel was surprised. 'Mr Ferrars is to be married?' he said. 'I am afraid that the curate's house at Delaford is not big enough for a married man. He will have to find a larger house. A marriage would not be possible for some time.'

As the Colonel stood up to leave, Mrs Jennings came into the drawing-room. She heard his last words with some surprise.

'Why is the Colonel not getting married at once?' the old lady thought. She decided to find out the truth from Elinor.

'Well, Miss Dashwood,' Mrs Jennings said after the Colonel had left the house, 'I know what you and the Colonel were talking about and I am very happy to hear your news.'

'Thank you, ma'am,' Elinor replied. 'The Colonel is very kind and he has surprised me very much.'

Mrs Jennings laughed. 'I am not surprised at all,' she said. 'And your friends will not be surprised either, when I tell them your good news.'

'Please do not talk about it to anyone, ma'am,' Elinor said quickly. 'I must write to Mr Ferrars first. I am going to do that now.' And she went to a desk in the corner of the room.

'A marriage would not be possible for some time.'

'Oh, I see!' Mrs Jennings said quietly to herself. 'Mr Ferrars must be ordained first. Elinor and Brandon want him to perform their marriage ceremony[59]!'

And so the old lady hurried out of the house, to pass on this piece of gossip to all her friends.

Elinor did not hear Mrs Jennings' words, because she was thinking about her letter to Edward. As she sat down to write, Edward himself came into the room.

The young people were both very surprised to see each other and they did not know what to say or do.

Edward sat in a chair and looked down at his hands. He was silent for several minutes before he began to speak.

'I apologise. You are busy. You are writing letters,' Edward said. 'I – I am sorry. I met Mrs Jennings as I came in. She said that you had something important to tell me.'

'I was just writing to you. I have some good news,' Elinor said with a smile. 'Colonel Brandon was here earlier. He has heard that you are being ordained. He wants to help you. He is offering you the position of a curate in Delaford.'

'Colonel Brandon wants to help me?' Edward said.

'Yes, he heard about your ... your problem and he wants to help you.'

'Colonel Brandon wants to help *me*?' Edward repeated. 'The Colonel is your friend, Elinor, not mine. You must be the reason for his kindness to me.'

'No, I said nothing to the Colonel,' Elinor told Edward. 'It was his idea, not mine.'

Edward stood up quickly. 'Then I must go and thank the Colonel at once,' he said. Then he bowed and left the room.

Elinor sighed. 'When I see dear Edward again, he will be married to Lucy Steele,' she thought.

Mrs Jennings returned soon after Edward's visit. She still thought that Elinor was going to marry Colonel Brandon. At first, Mrs Jennings was very disappointed when Elinor told her the truth. But the old lady was soon cheerful again and she talked happily about visiting Edward and Lucy in their new home.

Mrs Jennings then went and told this piece of news to her friends and soon everyone had their own ideas about it.

Mr and Mrs John Dashwood were very surprised by Colonel Brandon's kindness to Edward. John wanted to know how much money Edward would get every year. Fanny was angry and upset because Edward and Lucy would now be able to marry. John and Fanny decided not to tell Mrs Ferrars the news. They knew that she would be very angry.

Mr Robert Ferrars laughed when he heard the news. 'Poor Edward!' Robert said. 'What a dull life he will have as a poor clergyman! And he will be married to Lucy Steele too! How can they be happy without money? No one will want to know them now!'

13

Cleveland

In the first week of April, the Palmers, Mrs Jennings, the Miss Dashwoods and Colonel Brandon left London for Cleveland. The ladies rode in a carriage and they took Charlotte's baby with them. They arrived at Cleveland on the morning of the third day. Colonel Brandon and Mr Palmer rode horses and they followed more slowly.

Cleveland was a big fine house that was surrounded by pretty gardens and beautiful trees. For the first few days, the weather was fine and Marianne spent her time walking in the gardens.

Combe Magna, Willoughby's home, was thirty miles away.

But the house and its owner were always in Marianne's thoughts.

By the time that Colonel Brandon and Mr Palmer arrived, rain had started to fall. For several days it was so wet that they all had to stay indoors. The friends happily sat and talked to each other. In his own home, Mr Palmer was no longer rude. He was polite and kind to his visitors.

Colonel Brandon often talked to Elinor, but his eyes were often turned towards Marianne.

It was the Colonel who first noticed that Marianne was sick. She had gone for a walk where the grass was long and wet. Then she had come indoors and sat for too long in her wet shoes and stockings. She caught a cold[60].

Marianne went to bed early and she woke up the next day feeling tired and ill. By the evening, she had a fever[61] and the Palmers sent for their doctor.

The doctor came and looked at Marianne carefully. He touched her forehead. Her skin was very hot and her body was shaking. The doctor looked very worried.

'This young lady has a bad fever,' he said. 'You have a very young baby, Mrs Palmer. I suggest that you and your child leave Cleveland for a time. You do not want your baby to catch the fever too.'

Charlotte agreed and she left Cleveland the same day. She went to stay with some neighbours.

Mrs Jennings was worried about Marianne and she said that she would stay at Cleveland. Elinor was very pleased to have the kind old lady's help and they decided to look after Marianne together.

On the third day of Marianne's illness, Mr Palmer left Cleveland. He went to join his family at their neighbours' house. Colonel Brandon stayed at Cleveland so that he could offer his help. Marianne knew nothing about all this. She was too ill. She saw only Elinor, Mrs Jennings and the doctor, who came every day.

Three days later, when Marianne woke in the morning, she felt a little better. But that evening, she became much worse. By midnight, the poor girl was weeping and asking to see her mother. A servant was sent to get the doctor.

'Miss Marianne Dashwood is extremely ill,' the doctor said. 'Her mother should be here. Please send for her, Miss Dashwood. Your sister is in great danger.'

Elinor was very frightened and she ran downstairs to speak to Colonel Brandon.

'Oh! Colonel Brandon,' Elinor said with tears in her eyes. 'We need your help. My sister is very ill and the doctor says that our mother should be here.'

The Colonel stood up.

'I will leave for Barton at once,' he said. 'I can bring your mother here in about twenty-two hours. I shall be as quick as I can.'

In half an hour, a carriage and a pair of horses were ready and the Colonel was on his way to Barton.

The doctor called twice in the next ten hours. Each time that he came, Marianne was asleep and she was breathing very quickly. She could hear no one and she could see no one. She did not know who was beside her bed. Her fever was now at its worst.

When the doctor called at four o'clock in the afternoon, Marianne's breathing was slower and her skin was cooler. Once or twice, she opened her eyes. Elinor sat beside her poor sister's bed and held her hand.

At six o'clock, Marianne was in a deep, peaceful sleep. Elinor began to hope that her sister would get well.

At seven o'clock, Marianne was still sleeping comfortably. Elinor went downstairs to have tea with Mrs Jennings and to give her the good news. Then she went back to her sister's room and sat down by the bed once more. Colonel Brandon would not return with Mrs Dashwood until ten o'clock.

The night was cold and stormy. The wind blew and the rain fell. Marianne went on sleeping.

At eight o'clock, Elinor thought that she heard the sound of a carriage driving up to the house. She ran to the window, opened the wooden shutter, and looked out.

Yes, there were the lights of a carriage outside! But the carriage was being pulled by four horses, not two.

'That must be why Colonel Brandon has returned so quickly,' Elinor thought.

Elinor ran downstairs to see her mother and Colonel Brandon. She was smiling happily. Now everything would be well! She heard someone walking from the hallway to the drawing-room.

Elinor opened the door of the drawing-room and ran in. But her mother and Colonel Brandon were not standing in the room – it was Willoughby!

Elinor stopped. Her face became pale with shock. She had already turned back to the door, when Willoughby spoke.

'Miss Dashwood!' Willoughby cried. 'Give me time to explain why I am here. Please, stay and hear what I have to say!'

'No, sir,' Elinor said quickly. 'I shall not stay. I do not want to hear your explanation. Perhaps you have business with Mr Palmer. I am sorry, but he is away at the moment.'

'I do not know Mr Palmer and I have no business with him,' Willoughby said. 'I came as soon as I heard the terrible news about your sister. Please, let me explain why I am here, Miss Dashwood.'

Elinor sat down.

'Then please be quick, sir,' she said. 'My sister needs me and I have no time to talk to you.'

But her mother and Colonel Brandon were not standing in the room – it was Willoughby!

'The servant told me that your sister is now out of danger. Is that true? Is she a little better? For God's sake, tell me if that is true or not!' Willoughby cried. His face was pale and his eyes were wide and dark.

'We hope that it is true,' Elinor said quietly.

Willoughby stood up and began to walk about the room. Then he stopped and turned towards Elinor.

'Tell me, Miss Dashwood,' he said. 'What do you think about me? Am I bad or stupid?' He laughed suddenly. His face had now become red.

Willoughby was speaking very strangely. Elinor began to think that he was drunk.

'Mr Willoughby, I think that you should go home and rest,' Elinor said, frowning.

Willoughby understood.

'No, Miss Dashwood, I am not drunk,' he said. 'I have come here for a very good reason. I am very, very sorry. I have come here to make an apology and explain my behaviour to your sister. Perhaps, in time, she may even forgive me.'

'Marianne has already forgiven you,' Elinor replied. 'She forgave you long ago.'

'Then you must listen to me, Miss Dashwood. Last autumn, I had to spend some time in Devon – at Allenham Court, with Mrs Smith. Then I met your sister. Her interest in me was very flattering and I did my best to please her.'

'I have heard enough,' Elinor said coldly. 'I cannot listen to you any more.'

'But you must,' Willoughby replied. 'I have to tell you everything now.

'I am a gentleman, but I have never had much money of my own. My friends have always been much richer than me. When I was with them, I spent money freely and I soon had many debts[62].

'I was not going to inherit Mrs Smith's money for many

years, so I decided that I must marry a rich woman. I had no thought of marrying anyone like your sister. That was not possible. But Marianne is very beautiful and I began to grow very fond of her. I fell in love – I could not help it.'

'Then you did have feelings for Marianne,' Elinor said.

'The hours that I spent with your sister, were the happiest of my life,' Willoughby said. 'But then something happened that changed everything. Mrs Smith heard a story about me. She heard about someone – a lady – whom I ... But I believe that you have been told everything, Miss Dashwood,' Willoughby said.

'Yes, I have heard it all,' Elinor said angrily. 'You left a young, pregnant girl alone, and without money. You behaved very badly towards that poor girl. She had no one to help her. It was a wicked thing that you did.'

'Remember who told you that story!' Willoughby cried. 'Colonel Brandon is no friend of mine!'

'You should be ashamed[63]!' Elinor answered. 'You treated that girl badly and you treated my sister badly too. You deceived them. You flattered them and made them love you. Marianne loved you and she believed your flattery. By then, Eliza Williams had no hope and no friends. You knew that, but you did nothing to help her.'

'I did not know that Eliza was in trouble,' Willoughby said quickly. 'I had forgotten to give her my address and she could not write to me.

'Mrs Smith thought the worst of me too,' Willoughby went on. 'She is an old woman and she does not understand a young man's feelings. She said that she would forgive me, if I married Eliza. I could not do that. So Mrs Smith sent me away. She told me that I would never inherit her money.

'Miss Sofia Grey was very rich and I decided to marry her,' Willoughby said. 'She was pleased to get a husband. That is all. We do not love each other.'

'Miss Grey is now your wife,' Elinor said quietly. 'Please don't speak about her in that way. You have made two young women unhappy – first Eliza and then my poor sister. You were cruel to Marianne when you said goodbye to her at Barton. You were cruel to her again in London, in front of her friends and many other people. Your last letter to Marianne was the cruellest thing of all. You have not behaved like a gentleman, Mr Willoughby.'

'My wife made me write that letter,' Willoughby said. 'She was angry and jealous. Oh, why did I leave Marianne for her?'

'You have already told me why,' Elinor said. 'Do not say that your wife is the reason for your bad behaviour. Perhaps you have been foolish, rather than wicked. But you have hurt my sister terribly. She has been very unhappy.'

'Then please tell your sister that now I am unhappy too,' Willoughby replied. 'I still love Marianne. I came here tonight because I met Sir John Middleton in London. He told me that Marianne was dying. Mrs Jennings had written to tell him the news. You must tell Marianne everything that I have told you tonight.'

Willoughby stopped speaking and turned away. He looked so unhappy that Elinor felt sorry for him.

'Marianne will be happy one day, but I shall never be,' the young man added sadly. 'Goodbye.'

After saying these words, Willoughby left the room. In a few minutes, he was in his carriage and he was driving away from Cleveland.

Willoughby's visit had upset Elinor very much and it was some time before she could go upstairs again. When Elinor did go into Marianne's room, she found that her sister was much better. Elinor was delighted.

Thirty minutes later, Elinor heard the sound of another

carriage outside the house. Mrs Dashwood and Colonel Brandon had arrived at last! When the Colonel had reached Delaford, he had gone in his own carriage to Barton Cottage to bring Mrs Dashwood to Cleveland. The Colonel and Mrs Dashwood had travelled for many hours. Mrs Dashwood was now at the side of her dear daughter and she stayed with her all night.

Elinor went to bed, but she could not sleep. She had too much to think about. But she felt happier than she had been for some time.

A week passed and the Palmers returned to their home. Mrs Dashwood was happy to see Marianne get stronger every day. But she had another reason to be happy.

'Colonel Brandon loves our dear Marianne,' she told Elinor. 'He told me this as we travelled from Barton. I once thought that he would marry you, Elinor. But now I believe that he will suit Marianne better. He truly loves her. He loves her more than Willoughby ever could, I am sure of that.'

'Colonel Brandon is a good man,' Elinor replied. 'He has shown great kindness to all his friends. What did you say to the Colonel? Did you give him any hope for a future with Marianne?'

'I could not give him hope, because I thought that Marianne was dying,' Mrs Dashwood said. 'But in time, Marianne will understand that he is a far better man than Willoughby. It will take her some time to forget that young man, I know. But Colonel Brandon is patient – he will wait until Marianne grows fond of him. He has told me so.'

Marianne got better and stronger every day. Soon she was well enough to come out of her room and sit downstairs, in the drawing-room.

Colonel Brandon sat beside her and held her thin hand. He looked sadly at her thin, pale face as she thanked him for bringing her mother on the long journey from Barton.

A few days later, Mrs Dashwood said that Marianne was strong enough to leave Cleveland.

The Dashwoods thanked the Palmers and Mrs Jennings for all their kind help. Then they travelled home to Barton Cottage in the Colonel's carriage and Colonel Brandon rode back to Delaford on his horse.

14

The Return to Barton Cottage

As the Dashwoods got nearer to Barton, each field and each hill and each tree reminded them of everything that had happened since they had come to Devon. Some thoughts were happy and some were sad.

When they reached Barton Cottage, Elinor saw tears on her sister's face. But as soon as they went inside their little house, Marianne became more cheerful. She began to talk about the future.

'When I am stronger and the weather is better, we will all go on long walks,' Marianne told her sisters. 'I am going to make good use of my time. I will study. I will play the piano every day. I will read more too. I know that I can borrow books from Colonel Brandon's library at Delaford.'

Elinor smiled at her sister's words. She was pleased that Marianne was so much happier. Then Elinor remembered that she must soon tell Marianne about Willoughby's visit to Cleveland. She wanted to wait until Marianne was stronger, but a few days later Elinor's chance came.

The two girls were walking slowly up the hill behind the cottage, when Marianne stopped. She looked at the ground.

'That is the place where I fell,' Marianne said. 'It is the place where I first saw Willoughby.'

Marianne was silent for a moment and then she went on.

'I can say his name without weeping now,' she said. 'My feelings for him are very different. But is Willoughby wicked, Elinor? I wish that I knew. I behaved badly too. I understand that now. I have been very selfish. I have thought only about myself and my own feelings. But I think that I have changed now. Has Willoughby changed too? I shall never know.'

This was Elinor's chance. Very kindly and carefully, she began to tell her sister about Willoughby's visit to Cleveland. She told Marianne that Willoughby apologised for the way that he had treated her. And he was sorry that he had hurt her.

Marianne listened in silence. Tears ran down her face. After a few minutes, Elinor gently took her sister back to Barton Cottage.

'Elinor, tell mama that I know everything,' Marianne said quietly, as she went upstairs to her room.

Elinor told her mother everything about Willoughby. Mrs Dashwood had once liked Willoughby very much. She remembered the day that Willoughby left Barton. He had treated her daughter badly. He had been cruel and unkind to Eliza, and then to Marianne. Mrs Dashwood would never forgive the young man for deceiving both these young women. Colonel Brandon was now her favourite.

Marianne agreed with her mother. 'I could never have been happy with Willoughby,' she said.

Elinor knew how unhappy Willoughby was. But she also knew that he was more sorry for himself than for Marianne.

'Willoughby has always thought of himself first,' Elinor said to Marianne. 'He is sorry now, but only because he has lost you.'

The Dashwood's quiet life at Barton Cottage continued once again. Marianne was happier now, but Elinor was not. She thought a lot about Edward Ferrars. Elinor had heard that Edward had gone to Oxford. But no one knew anything more about him or what he was going to do.

Then, one day, news of Edward reached the Dashwoods. Thomas, the family's servant, had been to Exeter to buy food. When he returned, he spoke to Mrs Dashwood and her girls.

'I suppose that you know, ma'am, that Mr Ferrars is now married?' Thomas said.

Marianne looked at Elinor and saw that her sister's face had become pale. Elinor was sitting very still, looking down at the table in front of her.

'Who told you that Mr Ferrars was married, Thomas?' Mrs Dashwood asked quietly.

'I saw Mrs Ferrars myself, ma'am. She was in a carriage with her husband,' Thomas replied. 'Mrs Ferrars used to be Miss Lucy Steele, of course. When she saw me, she waved her hand in greeting. She told me that she had got married. She sent you all her best wishes, ma'am.'

'Did you say that Mr Ferrars was in the carriage with her?' Mrs Dashwood asked.

'Yes, ma'am, but he did not speak and I did not see him clearly. They were driving towards the west. Mrs Ferrars said that they would call here very soon.'

This was terrible news and all the Dashwoods were very upset. All of Elinor's hope for a marriage to Edward Ferrars had now gone.

'Edward and Lucy must have got married in London,' Mrs Dashwood said to Elinor. 'They will soon be living at Delaford. Someone is sure to write to us soon and tell us more.'

But no letter about the Ferrars' marriage came to Barton Cottage.

A few days later, the Dashwoods were expecting a visit from Colonel Brandon. Elinor was looking out of the window when she saw a man riding a horse along the road towards the cottage. She stood up.

'Here is Colonel Brandon, mama,' Elinor said. 'He will give us news of Edward, I am sure.'

Then Elinor looked towards the road again.

'Oh! It is not the Colonel. It is Edward himself!' she cried. Her face suddenly became very pale. She looked towards her mother, Margaret and Marianne, but no one spoke. They all waited in silence as Edward got off his horse, walked up the path, and came into the house.

Seconds later, Edward was in the sitting-room. He bowed to each of the Dashwoods. His face was as pale as Elinor's and he looked very uncomfortable. He was holding his hat and gloves and turning them over, again and again.

Mrs Dashwood stood up and held out her hand to the young man. 'We must give you our best wishes, Edward,' Mrs Dashwood said.

Edward said something in reply, but he spoke so quietly that no one could understand him. There was silence and then Elinor said something about the weather. There was silence again.

'Is Mrs Ferrars in Plymouth?' Elinor asked Edward at last.

Edward looked surprised at her question.

'No, my mother is in London,' he replied.

'I was speaking about Mrs *Edward* Ferrars,' Elinor said quietly. She could not look at Edward's face.

The young man looked more surprised than before.

'Perhaps you mean ... my brother has ... You must mean Mrs Robert Ferrars,' he said at last.

'Mrs *Robert* Ferrars?' said Mrs Dashwood and Marianne together.

Elinor did not speak, but she now looked at Edward's face.

He stood up and walked towards the window before he answered.

'You may not have heard the news,' he said. 'My brother, Robert, has married Miss Lucy Steele. They are now in the town of Dawlish. They are on their honeymoon[64].'

Elinor turned quickly and ran from the room. As soon as the door was shut behind her, she gave a cry and began to weep loudly. Elinor's tears were tears of happiness and she did not stop crying for a very long time.

Edward went back to his seat and sat there in silence. Mrs Dashwood asked him several questions, but he did not answer. At last, without saying a word, he stood up, bowed, and left the room. He hurried from the cottage and began to walk quickly towards the village.

A short time later, Edward returned to Barton Cottage and he found Elinor alone in the sitting-room.

'I came to Barton to see you, my dearest Elinor,' Edward said. 'At last I am free. And at last I can ask you to marry me. I shall never be a rich man, but, with you, I shall be a happy one. Can you be happy with me, Elinor?'

'Yes, dear Edward, oh, yes,' Elinor replied quietly. 'I have always loved you. You must know that!'

So, by the afternoon, Elinor and Edward were engaged, and the Dashwoods of Barton Cottage were happier than they had ever been before.

The marriage of Lucy to Robert Ferrars had been a surprise to everyone, including Edward himself. But the marriage meant that Edward was now able to tell Elinor about his love for her. Edward had behaved like an honest man and now he was a happy one too. Elinor could at last show her true feelings for her dear Edward and the Dashwoods happily welcomed Edward into their family.

She gave a cry and began to weep loudly.

Lucy had written a letter to Edward after her marriage to his brother. Edward showed the letter to Elinor.

Dear Sir,

When I understood that you no longer loved me, I felt that I was free. I could then give my love to another man. Your brother and I could not live without each other, so we got married. Robert and I are now on our way to Dawlish, for our honeymoon. I am sure that I will be happy with him and that he will be happy with me. I hope that, in the future, you will be happy too and that we shall be good friends. We are both members of the same family now.

I thought that I should write and tell you this news myself. I have burnt all your letters and I shall send back your picture, when I have time. You can keep the ring with the lock of my hair in it.

Your friend and sister-in-law,
Lucy Ferrars

'Well, I hope that they will be happy,' Elinor said, as she gave the letter back to Edward. 'But your mother will not be happy at all. She wanted to stop your marriage to Lucy, so she gave your brother your money. And now Robert has married Lucy himself! That will hurt your mother very much.'

'Robert's marriage will hurt my mother, but Robert has always been her favourite,' Edward said. 'Mother will soon forgive him. But will Robert and Lucy be happy together? I do not know.'

'Lucy is very sly and she is clever too,' Elinor said. 'You believed that she loved you. But I have known Lucy's true feelings for a long time. She wanted to marry a man from a good family. That was the most important thing for her.'

'I was nineteen years old when I first met Lucy Steele and became engaged to her,' Edward said. 'I soon found out that I did not love her. But I thought that it was wrong to end the engagement. I was poor. And I thought that Lucy was honest when she said that she loved me.'

'Any girl is happy to be engaged,' Elinor said with a smile. 'Your mother was very angry when she found out about your secret engagement. But Lucy hoped that she would forgive you and give you money.'

'Elinor, I admired you from the first time that I saw you at Norland,' Edward said. 'But I thought that my feelings were friendship, not love. By the time that I understood the truth, it was too late. I hurt you and made myself unhappy too.'

Elinor smiled.

'That unhappy time is past, my dear Edward,' she said. 'Now we must begin to think about our own future.'

Edward stayed at Barton Cottage as a welcome guest. He was delighted to hear that Colonel Brandon was coming to stay at Barton Park. Edward had not yet been to Delaford. He thanked the Colonel again for giving him the position of curate at Delaford. During Edward's stay, Colonel Brandon visited the cottage every day and the two gentlemen were soon good friends.

Elinor and Edward now began to think of how much money they would have when they were married. It was not much. Edward had £2000 of his own, and Elinor had £1000. Edward would receive £200 a year for his work at the church at Delaford.

Two letters arrived at Barton Cottage. They had both been written in London. One letter was from Mrs Jennings, and the other was from John Dashwood. They both gave the news about Lucy Steele's marriage to Robert Ferrars.

Mrs Jennings had written:

Poor Edward Ferrars! He has now gone to Oxford alone and he is very unhappy. Lucy Steele was sly! No one knew anything about her marriage to Robert Ferrars, not even her sister, Anne. Lucy borrowed all of Anne's money to buy wedding-clothes. Then she left Anne alone in London!

Perhaps you can invite Edward to Barton – then gentle and kind Miss Marianne will be able to comfort him.

John Dashwood's letter was longer and it was all about the feelings of Mrs Ferrars and of John's wife, Fanny. John had written:

Mrs Ferrars and my dear Fanny are both very upset by the news of Robert's marriage. Mrs Ferrars is very angry. She says that she never wants to hear the names of Robert or Lucy ever again.

Poor Fanny has wept all day for Mrs Ferrars' unhappiness and her own.

No one has heard any news from Edward, but we think that he is still in Oxford. I will write to him there. I will tell him to write to his sister, Fanny. He should apologise for his bad behaviour in the past. Fanny could then show the letter to her mother.

We all know how kind dear Mrs Ferrars is, and how she wants to be friends with both her sons. If Edward writes to Fanny now, it might help him in the future.

Elinor showed John Dashwood's letter to Edward. She thought that Edward should write to his sister.

'But I am *not* sorry for my behaviour!' Edward said. 'I am going to marry you and I am not sorry about that at all!'

'But perhaps you could say that you are sorry about your first engagement,' Elinor said. 'And then you could tell Fanny about your second engagement! In this way, your mother will know that we are to be married.'

Edward thought about this suggestion. He decided to go to London and speak to his mother himself.

A little later, Colonel Brandon and Edward Ferrars left Barton together. They went first to Delaford, to see the house where Edward was going to live when he became the curate. They made plans for some extra rooms to be built. Then Edward travelled to London, to see his mother and his sister.

15

Engagements and Marriages

Edward's visit to his mother went well. At first, Mrs Ferrars told her elder son about her anger and unhappiness. But then she forgave him.

Mrs Ferrars had given birth to two sons. Most of the Ferrars family's money should have been inherited by her elder son, Edward. But when Mrs Ferrars heard about Edward's secret engagement to Lucy Steele – an unsuitable woman with no money of her own – Mrs Ferrars refused to know Edward. She made arrangements for all the family's money to be inherited by Robert.

For a few months, Robert was her only son. Then Robert had married Lucy Steel and Mrs Ferrars refused to know either of her sons. Now she was friends with Edward and she had a son again.

Edward told his mother that Elinor Dashwood was soon going to be her daughter-in-law. He expected Mrs Ferrars to be angry once more, but he was surprised. Mrs Ferrars was not angry at all. Neither did she tell her son that Miss Morton – the rich daughter of a lord – would be a far better wife than Elinor Dashwood. Instead, she agreed to the marriage of

Edward and Elinor. And she also said that she would give them a wedding gift of £10,000!

Elinor and Edward were married in Barton church, early in the autumn. Then they travelled to Delaford in Dorset.

For the first month of their marriage, Edward and Elinor stayed with Colonel Brandon. While they were guests in his home, Edward and Elinor were able to plan all the changes to their little house beside the church. They moved into their new home as soon as the extra rooms had been built and the house had been decorated with new paint. In a short time, they were able to welcome their friends and family.

Mrs Dashwood and Margaret, Colonel Brandon, Mrs Jennings, and Sir John and Lady Middleton came to see them. John and Fanny Dashwood travelled from Sussex to Dorset to see them. Mrs Ferrars was also a visitor.

Although they warmly welcomed Mrs Ferrars to their new home, Edward and Elinor did not flatter her. However, Robert and Lucy did flatter her. They tried to make the old lady like them. Mrs Ferrars was soon friends with Robert again, and she gave them money too.

Shortly after this, Robert and Lucy went to live in Harley Street, in London. They became the neighbours of John and Fanny Dashwood. Lucy and Fanny often argued, but apart from that, they all lived in great happiness.

John Dashwood visited Colonel Brandon's home at Delaford. He thought that the house and its grounds were nearly as good as his own property, Norland Park. He told Elinor that the Colonel would make a fine husband for her sister, Marianne.

Marianne's family also thought that the Colonel should marry Marianne. Mrs Dashwood, Marianne and Margaret were often invited to Delaford. While they were there, the Colonel did everything to show his love for Marianne.

Marianne's opinion about Colonel Brandon had now changed.

When she was seventeen, she had thought that Colonel Brandon was too old to be married. But now, two years later, Marianne loved him with all her heart and she agreed to become his wife. They were married in the church at Delaford where Edward Ferrars was the curate.

Marianne was kind, loving and thoughtful. She worked hard in her new home. Very soon everyone loved the young wife of the owner of Delaford.

Willoughby was sorry that he had lost Marianne, but his own marriage was not always unhappy. And, after a time, old Mrs Smith forgave him and she made him her heir again.

After Elinor and Marianne's happy marriages, Mrs Dashwood lived at Barton Cottage with Margaret. Sir John Middleton invited Margaret to parties and dances at Barton Park where she met many suitable young men. Mrs Jennings was often a visitor in her son-in-law's house. And as in the past, the cheerful, kind-hearted old lady continued to tease the young people and talk about love and lovers.

Points for Understanding

1

Why do Mrs Dashwood and her daughters leave Norland Park?

2

Who lives in these houses?
(a) Barton Park (b) Barton Cottage (c) Allenham Court
(d) Delaford

3

How are these people related?
(a) John Dashwood and Mrs Dashwood (b) Sir John Middleton and Mrs Jennings (c) John Dashwood and Edward Ferrars
(d) Willoughby and Mrs Smith (e) Colonel Brandon and Miss Eliza Williams

4

Which events in this chapter make these people upset?
(a) Marianne (b) Willoughby (c) Edward (d) Elinor

5

Describe these characters. Are they like or unlike each other?
(a) Lady Middleton and Charlotte Palmer (b) Sir John Middleton and Thomas Palmer (c) Fanny Dashwood and Edward Ferrars
(d) Anne and Lucy Steele

6

The words *flattered*, *sly* and *frown* have been used in Chapters 5 and 6. Which characters:
(a) flatter someone
(b) behave in a sly way
(c) are teased for frowning?

7

Why do the Dashwood sisters have different feelings about Mrs Jennings' invitation to London?

8

Which words or phrases in Willoughby's letter to Marianne do you think are examples of cruelty and coldness?

9

Willoughby had behaved shamefully before he arrived at Barton. What had he done?

10

Give two examples of how money and marriage are discussed in this chapter.

11

How does the secret come out?

12

Who is:
(a) delighted by Colonel Brandon's offer (b) disappointed when she hears the truth about Brandon and Elinor (c) amused when he hears the news about Edward and Lucy?

13

What happens at Cleveland when:
(a) Marianne goes for a walk in the long, wet grass? (b) the doctor comes at midnight on the third day of the Dashwoods' stay?
(c) Elinor hears a carriage arrive at eight o'clock?

14

Which things upset Elinor in this chapter? What makes her happy?

15

1 What is the difference between someone who has 'sense' and someone who has 'sensibility'?
2 At the beginning of the story, which characters have sense, and which characters have sensibility?
3 How have they now changed?

Glossary

1 ***county*** (page 4)
the United Kingdom of Great Britain is made up of England, Scotland, Wales and Northern Ireland. Each of these areas are divided into smaller areas called *counties*. See the map on page 7. The land outside towns, where there are farms, trees, mountains and lakes, is called *the countryside*. This word is often shortened to *the country*.

2 ***clergyman*** (page 4)
a Christian priest. A *curate* works in a church with a *clergyman*. They look after the church and the people who go there to pray.

3 ***parks*** (page 4)
places in towns where people can sit, walk and play games. There are usually trees and gardens of flowers in *parks*. Sometimes there are lakes. In the nineteenth century, large houses in the country were often surrounded by parks. 'Park' is also sometimes used as the name of a house or property. For example: *Norland Park*.

4 ***relatives*** (page 4)
members of a family – particularly those members who do not live together.

5 ***changed her mind*** – *to change your mind* (page 5)
decide to do something different, or to make a new plan. Jane first agreed to marry Mr Bigg-Wither, then she made a decision not to marry him. She *changed her mind*.

6 ***inherit*** – *to inherit* (page 5)
receive money or property from someone who has died. The money or property that a person receives is their *inheritance*.

7 ***visiting card*** (page 5)
a small card with your name printed on it.

8 ***suitable*** (page 6)
in the nineteenth century, parents believed that it was important for their children to marry well. If their children's husbands or wives came from rich and powerful families, these were *suitable* marriages. A young man and a young woman who both came from good families, both had a good education, and who both liked the same things were *suited* to each other.

9 ***heir*** (page 10)
a person who will receive money or property when another person dies.

10 ***will*** (page 10)
a document which explains what someone wants to happen to their money and property after they die.

11 ***fond of*** – *to be fond of someone* (page 10)
to like and care for someone very much because you know them well.

12 ***funeral*** (page 11)
a ceremony that takes place after someone dies. After the *funeral*, the body of the dead person is buried in the ground, or it is burnt in a fire – it is cremated.

13 ***stepmother*** (page 11)
when a man who has children marries again, his wife becomes *stepmother* to his children. The children are her *stepchildren*.

14 ***dependent*** – *to be dependent on someone* (page 12)
if you are *dependent* on someone, you need them because they give you money to live. An *independent* person is someone who makes decisions about their life. They also have strong feelings about the things that they like or dislike.

15 ***persuaded*** – to persuade (page 12)
make someone think or do something because of what you say to them.

16 ***mama*** (page 12)
the word that a son or daughter uses for his or her mother. *Ma'am* is a shortened form of *madam* – a polite way of talking to a woman in the nineteenth century.

17 ***remain friends with*** – *to remain friends with someone* (page 12)
although Fanny has been very unkind to Mrs Dashwood and her daughters, Elinor thinks that they should stay a little longer at Norland. She thinks that they should learn more about John before they find a new home. Then they should continue to be pleasant to him and be interested in his life and his family.

18 ***live very cheaply*** (page 13)
spend only a little money on food, your home, etc.

19 ***china, linen*** (page 13)
things which are used in a house. Plates, cups and saucers are *china*. Bedsheets, pillows and cloths that cover tables are *linen*.

20 ***neighbourhood*** (page 14)
a *neighbour* is a person who lives near you. The area around your home is the *neighbourhood*.

21 ***charming*** (page 16)
pleasant and very attractive.
22 ***sighed*** – *to sigh* (page 16)
the soft sound that someone makes because they are sad, or tired, or disappointed.
23 ***It is a pity*** (page 16)
words that you say when you are disappointed about something.
24 ***share*** – *to share* (page 16)
two people who have the same feelings and the same thoughts about something, *share* those feelings and thoughts.
25 ***taste and opinions*** (page 16)
taste is the kind of things that you like. Your favourite kinds of art, books, music or clothes are examples of your taste. *Opinions* are your thoughts about someone or something. If you *have a good opinion of someone*, you like them, and you think that they are a good person.
26 ***real gentleman*** (page 16)
gentleman was the word used in the nineteenth century for a man from polite society. See the Note on page 5. A *real gentleman* was a man who had good manners. He was always polite and honest and he cared for other people's feelings.
27 ***profession*** (page 16)
a job for which you need special training. Teaching, medicine and law are the *professions* of teachers, doctors and lawyers.
28 ***rent*** – *to rent* (page 18)
if you pay money to live in another person's house, you are *renting* the house. The *rent* is the money that you pay each year, or each month, or each week.
29 ***member of Parliament*** (page 21)
Parliament is the group of politicians who make the laws in Britain. Each *member of Parliament* has been elected by the people.
30 ***teased*** – *to tease* (page 21)
say something to someone which makes them feel uncomfortable or angry. You *tease* someone because you want to have fun. Mrs Jennings is not unkind when she teases people. However, *teasing* can sometimes be cruel or unkind.
31 ***praised*** – *to praise* (page 22)
tell someone that they have done something very well.
32 ***admired*** – *to admire* (page 23)
if you like the way that someone or something looks, works, or behaves, you *admire* that person or thing.

You have *admiration* for someone because you think that they are attractive or clever.

33 ***shelter*** – *to shelter* (page 23)
find a safe, dry place to stay during bad weather.

34 ***bowed*** – *to bow* (page 24)
bend your head and the top part of your body towards someone when you meet them. *Bowing* was the polite way that men greeted someone in the nineteenth century.

35 ***rescued*** – *to rescue* (page 24)
help someone who has a problem, or save them because there is danger. A *rescuer* is someone who saves another person.

36 ***dull*** (page 28)
not interesting or exciting. Boring.

37 ***lock*** (page 30)
a small piece of a person's hair.

38 ***brother-in-law*** (page 31)
the brother of your husband or wife. An *in-law* is someone who you are related to by marriage.
For example: Edward Ferrars is John Dashwood's *brother-in-law*. Henry Dashwood was Fanny Dashwood's *father-in-law*. Mrs Jennings is Sir John Middleton's *mother-in-law*. Thomas Palmer is Mrs Jennings' *son-in-law*, etc.

39 ***curricle*** (page 34)
a small carriage which is pulled by two horses. *Curricles* had tall wheels and they could travel at great speed. Curricles were the favourite vehicles of young men in the nineteenth century.

40 ***quarrelled*** – *to quarrel* (page 38)
argue with someone who you know well.

41 ***fault*** – *to be someone's fault* (page 38)
when you do something which makes a problem for another person, *it is your fault* that they have the problem.

42 ***expecting a child*** – *to expect a child* (page 44)
going to have a baby. To be pregnant.

43 ***frowned*** – *to frown* (page 47)
move your eyebrows down and closer together. People *frown* because they are angry, or worried, or thinking carefully.

44 ***vulgar*** (page 48)
a way of speaking and behaving which is not polite. A *vulgar* person does not have a good education and they do not care about other people's feelings.

45 ***sly*** (page 48)
a *sly smile*, or a *sly remark* is a way of looking or speaking which shows that you know something that another person does not know.
A *sly person* is clever at tricking people. Or they might do unfair or dishonest things.

46 ***flattered*** – *to flatter* (page 50)
a way of speaking to someone so that they like you and they do what you want.
Flattery is telling someone that they are very clever, or that something which belongs to them is very good.

47 ***trusted*** – *to trust* (page 50)
show someone that you believe they are honest, kind and helpful.

48 ***tutor*** (page 50)
a teacher who does not work in a school. *Tutors* usually teach only a few students, and they teach them privately.

49 ***For God's sake*** (page 62)
a very strong way of asking why something is happening.

50 ***treated ... badly*** – *to treat someone badly* (page 65)
do or say something to someone that hurts them, or makes them unhappy.

51 ***divorced*** – *to be divorced* (page 71)
no longer be married because a judge in a court has agreed that the marriage has ended.

52 ***seduced*** – *to seduce* (page 72)
the way that someone behaves or speaks so that another person will have sex with them.

53 ***deceived*** – *to deceive* (page 72)
Willoughby made Eliza, and then Marianne, fall in love with him because he behaved in a loving way. But he never told them that he loved them. And he never asked either of them to be his wife. Willoughby *deceived* them by behaving dishonestly.

54 ***duel*** (page 72)
a fight between two men who use guns or swords. Gentlemen often fought *duels* because one man had done or said something bad to the other man. By the nineteenth century, it was against the law to fight a duel.

55 ***screens*** (page 79)
flat pieces of furniture which are used to separate one part of a room from another.

56 ***fainted*** – *to faint* (page 88)
suddenly fall to the ground because you are ill or have had a shock. Someone who *faints* cannot see or hear for a short time.

57 ***ordained*** – *to be ordained* (page 91)
a person has to take part in a special ceremony – be *ordained* – before they can become a priest or a clergyman.

58 ***position*** (page 94)
a job.

59 ***perform their marriage ceremony*** (page 96)
when a clergyman speaks special words at the marriage of a man and a woman, he is *performing a marriage ceremony*.

60 ***caught a cold*** – *to catch a cold* (page 98)
become ill after you had been wet and cold for too long.

61 ***fever*** (page 98)
a person who has a *fever* feels ill and the temperature of their body is very high.

62 ***debts*** (page 102)
amounts of money that someone owes to another person.

63 ***ashamed*** – *to be ashamed* (page 103)
have a bad feeling because you have done something wrong or you have been unkind to someone.

64 ***honeymoon*** (page 110)
a man and a woman who have just got married have a holiday called a *honeymoon*.

Exercises

Story Outline

Complete the gaps. Use each word (or phrase) in the box once.

Promise	thought	~~rich~~	generations	never	nephew
together	marriage	son	money	stated	take care of
inherit	twice	became	fond	altered	rest
until	died	estate	situation	owner	daughters
grounds					

Old Mr Dashwood was a [1]......*rich*...... man and the [2].................................... of Norland Park. The house and [3]... had been in the family for several [4].. .

Old Mr Dashwood [5].. married. He invited his [6]... Henry to live at Norland Park [7]... with his wife and children. Henry had married [8]....................................... . His son by his first [9]... was grown up and had a [10].................................. of his own – young Harry. Old Mr Dashwood [11]... very fond of this child; so [12]..............................., in fact, that he [13]... his will: he left his entire [14]... to four-year old Harry. Then old Mr Dashwood died; but that did not alter the [15]... at Norland Park.

Henry had three [16]... by his second marriage. They all lived together at Norland Park and [17]... of the house as their own. Indeed, old Mr Dashwood [18]... in his will that Henry could live there for the [19].. of his life.

All was well [20].. Henry fell sick. A few days before he [21].., he spoke to his son John: 'You must [22].. your step-mother and your sisters,' he said. 'They will have very little [23].. and your son will [24].. Norland Park. [25].. me you will take care of your mother and sisters.'

Words From The Story 1

Write each word from the box next to the correct meaning.

estate situation nephew state fond promise
alter think of ~~generations~~ rest

1 lifetimes	*generations*
2 the son of a brother or sister	
3 all of someone's property	
4 to like/love very much	
5 change	
6 set-up or things that are happening	
7 consider	
8 say exactly (in writing or speaking)	
9 remainder	
10 to say you will do something:	

Comprehension

Answer the questions.

Q1 What was the name of the Dashwood family home?
Norland Park..

Q2 Who did old Mr Dashwood make his heir?

....

Q3 Who did Elinor fall in love with?

....

Q4 What county did Mrs Dashwood and her daughters move to?

....

Q5 What is the name of the old lady who likes to gossip?

....

Q6 Who did Marianne fall in love with?

....

Q7 Where did Elinor and Marianne spend Christmas?

....

Q8 What did Edward Ferrars want to do for a living?

....

Q9 Who gave Edward Ferrars his job?

....

Q10 Who did Lucy Steele marry?

....

Word Focus

Write full sentences using *need* and *need to be*.

Example	*You must look after your sisters.*
need	Your sisters need looking after.
need to be	Your sisters need to be looked after.

1 You must take care of your sisters.
need ....
need to be ....

2 You must protect your sisters.
need ....
need to be ....

3 You must comfort your mother.
need ....
need to be ....

4 You must pay the servants.
need ....
need to be ....

5 You must alter the house.
need ....
need to be ....

6 You must follow the lawyer's advice.
need ....
need to be ....

Making Sentences

Write questions for the answers.

Example	***How*** *much did John propose giving to his sister?*
ANSWER	John proposed giving his sisters a thousand pounds each.

Q1 *Who*
A1 Fanny objected to John giving money away.

Q2 *Why*
A2 John proposed giving money to his sisters because he had promised his father.

Q3 *What*
A3 Fanny's objection was that the money belonged to their son Harry.

Q4 *When*
A4 Young Harry would inherit Norland Park at the age of 21.

Q5 *Why*
A5 Mrs Dashwood felt uncomfortable because she was a guest in her own house.

Q6 *Where*
A6 Mrs Dashwood and her daughters moved to Barton Cottage.

Q7 *Who*
A7 Sir John Middleton owned Barton Cottage.

Q8 *How many*
A8 Mrs Dashwood required only three servants at Barton Cottage.

Q9 Where
A9 Barton Cottage was situated in Devon.

Q10 *What*
A10 Mrs Jennings was Sir John Middleton's mother-in-law.

Grammar Focus

Write nouns for the verbs.

VERB	NOUN	VERB	NOUN
1 object	*objection*	11 inherit	
2 own		12 marry	
3 invite		13 die	
4 state		14 promise	
5 alter		15 consider	
6 require		16 propose	
7 situate		17 persuade	
8 sign		18 rent	
9 flatter		19 trust	
10 deceive		20 perform	

Pronunciation

Circle the word that sounds the same.

1	sign	light	sing	(line)	Spain	sir
2	heir	hear	air	hire	heart	heat
3	debt	bet	beat	bait	bite	boat
4	own	brown	whom	house	drown	stone
5	move	love	mauve	drove	groove	mud

Words From The Story 2

Unjumble the letters to find words that complete the sentences.

1 SEATTE — Old Dashwood left all his property to Harry.
He left his entire ...*estate*... to Harry.

2 TUNCOY — Devon is an administrative area in England.
Devon is an English ....

3 KRAP — The house was surrounded by gardens and trees and grass.
The house was situated in a ....

4 SILVEATER — John and Fanny are members of our family.
They are our ....

5 RITHEIN — Harry will become the owner of Norland Park when he is 21.
Harry will .... Norland Park.

6 BESTUIAL — Fanny did not believe that it was right and proper for a Dashwood girl to marry her brother.
She thought that such a marriage was not
....

7 HIRE	Henry believed that he would inherit old Mr Dashwood's estate. He thought that he was Mr Dashwood's ....
8 UNFLEAR	All the Dashwoods attended the burial service. They all went to the ....
9 TENPENDED	Mrs Dashwood had to rely on John for whatever money he would give her. She was .... on John.
10 SUPEADERD	Elinor made Mrs Dashwood change her mind and stay a little longer. Elinor .... Mrs Dashwood to stay.
11 SHIGOBRUNE	Sir John said: 'We live only half a mile away.' 'We are ....'
12 GINMARCH	Marianne wanted to marry a handsome and interesting man. She wanted her husband to be ....
13 NEGMANTLE	Willoughby was polite and well bred. He was a real ....
14 DEATES	Mrs Jennings made Elinor and Marianne feel awkward. She asked about their young men. 'I shall find out all your secrets soon,' she said. Mrs Jennings .... them with questions.
15 HERLETS	Margaret and Marianne got wet because there was nowhere to hide from the rain. There was no ....

16 SCUREED	Willoughby saved Marianne from the mud and the rain and carried her home. Willoughby .... Marianne.
17 LAUFT	'Mr Willoughby has had to go to London. But do not blame him.' It is not Mr Willoughby's ....
18 LERDTAFTE	She tried to be nice to the Middletons, but she was not always honest. She told them that they were charming and interesting people. She .... the Middletons.
19 DEVICEDE	Willoughby did not tell Marianne the truth. Colonel Brandon said: 'He has .... you.'
20 INTOPSOI	Colonel Brandon offered Mr Ferrar a job in the church. He offered him a ....
21 HEADSAM	'You treated that girl badly. You did not tell her the truth.' 'You should be .... of yourself.

Note: British / American spelling: neighbour / neighbor; colour / color; harbour / harbor etc.

Published by Macmillan Heinemann ELT
Between Towns Road, Oxford OX4 3PP
Macmillan Heinemann ELT is an imprint of
Macmillan Publishers Limited
Companies and representatives throughout the world
Heinemann is a registered trademark of Harcourt Education, used under license.

ISBN 1–405–05850–1
EAN 978–1–405058–50–6

This version of *Sense and Sensibility* by Jane Austen was retold by
Elizabeth Walker for Macmillan Readers
First published 2005

This version first published 2005

Illustrations by Ruth Palmer
Cover image by Bridgeman Gallery/Getty

Printed in Spain by Edelvives

2009 2008 2007 2006 2005
10 9 8 7 6 5 4 3 2 1